Praise for the Raine Stockton Dog Mystery Series

"An exciting, original and suspense-laden whodunit... A simply fabulous mystery starring a likeable, dedicated heroine..."
--*Midwest Book Review*

"A delightful protagonist...a well-crafted mystery."
--*Romantic Times*

"There can't be too many golden retrievers in mystery fiction for my taste."
--*Deadly Pleasures*

" An intriguing heroine, a twisty tale, a riveting finale, and a golden retriever to die for. [This book] will delight mystery fans and enchant dog lovers."
---*Carolyn Hart*

"Has everything--wonderful characters, surprising twists, great dialogue. Donna Ball knows dogs, knows the Smoky Mountains, and knows how to write a page turner. I loved it."
--*Beverly Connor*

"Very entertaining… combines a likeable heroine and a fascinating mystery… a story of suspense with humor and tenderness."
--*Carlene Thompson*

Other books in the Raine Stockton Dog Mystery series:

Smoky Mountain Tracks
Rapid Fire
Gun Shy
Bone Yard (a novella)
Silent Night

THE DEAD SEASON

A Raine Stockton Dog Mystery Book 6

By Donna Ball

Published by Blue Merle Publishing
Drawer H
Mountain City, Georgia 30562
www.bluemerlepublishing.com
ISBN 13: 978-0977329649
First printing May 2012

*This is a work of fiction. All places, characters,
events and organizations mentioned in this book are either
the product of the author's imagination, or used fictitiously.*

Cover by Sapphire Designs
http://designs.sapphiredreams.org/

This book is also available for your e-reader

CHAPTER ONE

The only good thing about a police interrogation room is that it's marginally better than a hospital emergency room. But neither is designed to be particularly warm or welcoming, and if I'd had my choice, they both would make my list of the Top Five Places I'd rather not be.

When the officer escorted me from the hospital to the waiting squad car, the first thing I said was, "Where is my dog?"

"I'll check into that for you, ma'am."

The sidewalk had been recently swept of snow and salted, but it was still slippery, and when I pulled away from his supporting hold on my elbow, I almost fell. He quickly caught my arm again. "I'm not talking to anyone until I see him," I told him forcefully. "Do you understand that? So you may as well take me to him right now."

"My orders are to drive you to the station," he said, not unkindly. "But like I said, I'll see what I can do."

I got into the back of the car because I had no choice, and at least it was warm inside. In the four hours I'd been in the emergency room, I had had a shower and a hot meal, and someone had even found a pair of clean scrubs for me, but I was still cold. I pulled my battered jacket around me and tried not to shiver. It was filthy, blood-stained, and smelled like smoke, but for five days it had kept me from freezing to death. Now it did little to alleviate the chill. I guess that's because the cold I felt came from the inside.

I leaned forward against the steel mesh divider as he started the car and demanded in a sudden panic, "They didn't take him to the animal shelter, did they?"

"No ma'am. I'm sure they didn't do that." He glanced at me in the rearview mirror. "Some of the kids were saying that dog was a real hero out there."

I leaned back wearily against the seat and watched the dirty snow banks go by with blank, unseeing eyes. "They all were," I said. "They all were heroes." I swallowed hard and added, "They said I couldn't see them at the hospital. The kids, I mean."

"Standard procedure, ma'am. We'll be taking your statements separately."

I knew that. I should have known that. I insisted, "But they're all right?"

"My understanding is that everyone who was brought in checked out fine. Some of their parents have already arrived. Others are on their way."

"That's good." I released a shaky breath and tried to unknot the tension in my shoulders. "That's good."

I added after a moment, "My husband is the sheriff of Hanover County in North Carolina."

That was not strictly true. In the first place, Buck Lawson was my ex-husband. In the second place, he was only acting sheriff. But I would have said I was married to God if it had meant a chance to see Cisco sooner.

The very polite deputy simply replied, "Yes, ma'am. I know."

When the car stopped and he opened the back door for me, I put my hand atop his and I said with quick, quiet urgency, "His name is Cisco. He's a golden retriever. He's a therapy dog, and a search and rescue dog. He helps people… he helps people," I finished simply, and by this time, I was pleading. "Don't let anything bad happen to him. Please."

The young officer's eyes gentled, and he said, "Yes, ma'am. Don't worry. I won't."

~

The Bullard County, South Carolina, Public Safety Building was not that much different from the sheriff's office in my hometown of Hansonville, North Carolina: ringing phones, linoleum floors, institutional green walls. But when I walked into the sheriff's office in Hansonville, two or three people would have greeted me with an easy, "Hey, Raine" before I got halfway into the building, and I didn't need a uniformed escort to take me where I was going.

But I wasn't at home anymore.

The officer opened the door of an interview room. "Detective Ritchie will be with you in a moment," he said. "Can I get you a coffee?"

I shook my head, then changed my mind. I had started to shiver again. "Yeah. Black. Thanks."

A man with thick, wavy gray hair, wire-rimmed glasses and an expensive-looking business suit came around the table toward me as I entered the room, his hand extended. "Miss Stockton," he said. "My name is Bryson Willis. I'm an attorney. Miles Young asked me to meet you here."

I stared at him, my head buzzing with four or five different questions, not knowing which of them to voice first. "But—I don't need an attorney," I said. "I didn't do anything. Anyway, I have an attorney. Sonny Brightwell—well, really she's my friend. She just says she's my attorney when something serious is going on."

His expression was somber. "Miss Stockton, there has been a murder. Something serious is definitely going on."

I swallowed hard. "Two," I said. "Two murders."

That grim expression in his eyes did not change. "Yes. Well, that's why we're here, isn't it?" He gestured for me to be seated at the table. "I've called Ms. Brightwell. She's on her way, but the roads are still bad and it may take awhile. If it's okay with you, I'll stand in her stead until she arrives."

I was alarmed. "No, don't call Sonny. She's on vacation. I don't want her driving all the way up here." But then I looked closely at his face and my throat went dry. "Am I in trouble? Have I been accused of something? Am I under arrest?"

"No," he assured me. "You're not under arrest. And my job is to see that you remain that way. There have been a lot of conflicting versions of what happened on that mountain. The police will be giving a lot of weight to your statement, since you were in the best position to witness everything that happened. So before we begin, I need to ask you—is there anything you would like to tell me about the events of the past week that may not necessarily make it into the statement you make to the police?"

I stared at him. "No. What do you mean?" Then more forcefully, "No."

His nod was neutral. "The first thing I want you to know is that we can postpone this interview until you've rested, if you want me to. We understand what you all went through out there. The police won't let you go home, but I can find you a hotel room…"

I was already shaking my head as I pulled out a chair and sank into it. "No, I just want to get this over with. Where is my dog? Can you find out where they took my dog?"

He sat down across from me. "The local vet is holding on to him for the time being. He checked him over and says he's doing fine. You'll be able to see him shortly."

I relaxed for the first time since I'd watched them strap Cisco into the harness and lift him into the air toward the hovering helicopter some six hours earlier. I drew in my breath for another question, and then the door opened and Detective Ritchie came in. I remembered him from the hospital, where I had given him a sketchy version of the events of the past forty-eight hours. He was accompanied by a younger man I had never met before. Both wore sports coats and dark trousers. Detective Ritchie wore a wool sweater under his coat; the other man wore a dark shirt.

Ritchie said, "Miss Stockton, this is Special Agent Leonard Brown from the FBI, who'll be sitting in with us. There's some issue about jurisdiction, since we seem to have a crossover of state lines, and some confusion about what took place where. We're hoping you can clear that up for us."

I nodded, although there was a cold lump in my stomach. I had dealt with the FBI before. I said, "My father was a judge. I understand." I sounded a lot more confident than I felt.

Detective Ritchie had two tall paper cups of coffee in his hand, and he passed one to me with a smile. "You're Roe Bleckley's niece, aren't you?" He turned to the other man and explained, "Roe was the sheriff down in Hanover County for thirty-odd years. I used to go fishing with him, back in the day. We liberated many a trout from the Tuckasegee once upon a time." He looked back at me. "I heard he retired. That right?"

The television cop shows would have you believe that all police detectives are hard-nosed bad-asses, who basically want to prosecute anyone who crosses their path; the truth is that, around these parts at least, they're mostly just regular guys doing their jobs. They know your grandma and go to church with your brother-in-law and, now and again, go fishing with your uncle, the neighboring sheriff.

While he pulled out his chair and settled in comfortably, I said, "That's right. He retired last fall."

He uncapped his coffee. "Who's running things over your way now?"

"My" — I started to say "husband" and caught myself. "Buck Lawson. He was the senior deputy when my uncle retired." Then I felt like an idiot because of course he knew who the sheriff of Hanover County was; it was only twenty miles away. He was just trying to be friendly, and give me an opportunity to establish my credentials. His patient look invited me to go on, so I added, "Buck is my former husband. He's in Florida now."

He nodded and sipped his coffee. "Yeah, I know. We tried to call him. Well, you tell your uncle I said hey, okay?" He glanced at the attorney, Mr. Willis. "Y'all ready?"

Mr. Willis nodded and the other man, Special Agent Brown, took out a yellow legal pad and flipped a switch on a box in the middle of the table. "Miss Stockton, we'll be videotaping this interview, if that's all right with you."

I nodded and sipped my coffee. It tasted a couple of days old, but it was hot and strong, and welcome to me.

"Please speak up."

I said, "Yes. It's fine." But I was starting to feel a little uncomfortable about the whole thing. I glanced at Mr. Willis for reassurance, but he was busy writing something down and didn't notice.

The agent added, with every pretense of friendliness, "I guess this is old-hat for you. You've been interviewed by the FBI before, haven't you, Miss Stockton?" He flipped a page on his yellow pad and glanced at it. "Last fall, I believe."

Before I could answer, Mr. Willis said, without glancing up, "I think we all acknowledge that Miss Stockton's work has put her in a position to be of help to the police many times before. And this is not an FBI interview, Agent Brown, so I don't see the relevance of what she was or was not doing last fall to the statement she is about to give now."

Detective Ritchie glanced at the FBI agent with a quirk of his eyebrow that seemed to say *Nice try* and then said to me, "Please state your name, age, address and occupation for the record."

I said, "My name is Raine Stockton, and I'm thirty six years old. I live at 101 Highway 11 East, Hanover, North Carolina. I own Dog Daze Boarding and Training in Hanover."

"You train dogs for a living?"

"I also work part time for the forest service. That's how I got involved in Search and Rescue."

Ritchie nodded and consulted the notes on his pad. "I know it's been a long day for you. We'll try not to keep you much longer."

"A long week," I said. I took another sip of my coffee. "It's been a long week."

He nodded sympathetically. "Let's get started, shall we?"

I said, "When can I see my dog?"

He glanced at Mr. Willis. "Soon," he said. "Real soon. Now, why don't you start at the beginning?"

I felt every muscle in my body tense up. I looked at Mr. Willis. He nodded encouragingly. I took a breath and released it as evenly as possible. "Right," I said. The sooner I got started, the sooner I could go home. The sooner I could get Cisco and just… go home. "From the beginning."

CHAPTER TWO

The first time I ever heard of the New Day Wilderness Program was when that kid, Brian Maddox, called me last October, wanting to know if I could give his dog what he called a "Good Canine Dog Test." Apparently, he had found my number in the yellow pages under "Dog Trainers." Since mine is the only dog training listing in the Hanover County and Surrounding Areas Telephone Directory–Raine Stockton, Dog Daze Boarding and Training, member APDT, certified CGC evaluator—the choice was a fairly easy one. Clearly, he had not gone to my website, or he would have known there is no such thing as a "Good Canine Dog Test."

I'm very proud of the website for Dog Daze, mostly because it took me almost a year to learn how to build it. There are all kinds of good things on the site, including a schedule of classes, photos of our graduates and all of their ribbons, my own gorgeous dogs, of course, with a complete list of all their accomplishments—and a full description of the Canine Good Citizen test.

It took me awhile to figure out that, that was, in fact, what Brian was referring to: the AKC's Canine Good Citizen test, which is a fairly simple ten-point examination to determine whether or not your dog has general good manners and whether he can maintain those manners in public under moderately stressful conditions.

According to Brian (who was really a very polite and articulate young man despite the fact he had obviously never heard of the Canine Good Citizen test until someone told him he should call me about it), his employer would let him bring his dog to work with him only if the dog was a certified therapy dog, or a Canine Good Citizen. He went on to explain that he worked for the New Day Wilderness Program, and that he was going into the wilderness for two weeks in three days and he didn't want to leave his dog behind, and asked if I could I do the test that day.

If he had gone to my website, he would've seen that I give the test four times a year, and that the last testing date had already passed. He was devastated. Wasn't there anything I could do for him? Did I know of anyone else in the area who did the test?

So I sent him to my website and told him to follow the link to the AKC's Canine Good Citizen page, where he could request a list of evaluators.

Five minutes later, he called back, wanting to know if he could pay extra to have me do the test right away. I tried to explain to him that the CGC test is considered something of a public service, and that the AKC frowns upon its evaluators trying to make a profit from it. Furthermore, it really made no sense to give the test for just one dog, since the entire point was to evaluate how the dog behaved around crowds and other canines. However, I told him to keep in touch, and that if I had enough students interested in taking the test I would schedule another one at the end of the month.

As it turned out, I did have three other people who wanted to test their dogs, so I was able to set up a test for two weekends away. I e-mailed Brian, and a couple of days later, he replied enthusiastically that he was leaving his dog with his girlfriend while he went into the wilderness, but he would be returning the day before the test and would definitely be able to make it.

And that was the last I—or anyone else, as it turned out—heard from him.

My life had been pretty full since then, and I completely forgot about the incident until a rainy day in the middle of January, when a girl named Heather McBane called to ask whether I did therapy dog certifications. She was also going into the wilderness in a couple of days and wanted to take her dog with her.

And that's how I got involved in what would turn out to be the biggest disaster of my life.

CHAPTER THREE

I love winter in the mountains. I love the way the soft cool light turns the distant mountains to lavender and reflects off the white-frosted ridge lines. I love waking up in the morning to find animal tracks in the snow outside my window, and I love the sound of white water tumbling through swollen streams and waterfalls. I love hiking with the dogs though miles and miles of silent woodlands, and coming unexpectedly upon sweeping vistas that never would have been visible in the spring or summer. I love the smell of wood smoke and curling up in a big chair in the evening with a good book and dogs piled all around me. Sometimes I think if we didn't have the winter to rest, we probably wouldn't survive the rest of the year.

Not much happens around here in between January and March. The sun doesn't clear the mountaintops until around nine a.m. and sets a little after five, so nobody expects to get much done. We drink a lot of coffee, chop a lot of kindling, and watch a lot of reruns of the old *Andy Griffith Show* on television. Andy, being a native, is huge in North Carolina, and at least two of the local stations are running an episode of the show at any given time.

The truth is, our little town of Hansonville, North Carolina, today is not all that different from Mayberry of the 1960s–or at least it seems that way in the winter time. If you go downtown on a January morning, yours is likely to be the only moving vehicle on the street, and you'd be hard-pressed to go into a shop or place of business without seeing someone you know. And if you dash across the street against the light in front of a law enforcement officer, he's more likely to help you carry your bags than give you a ticket, just like in Mayberry.

Of course, in my own case, that might be because, up until recently, my Uncle Roe had been the sheriff of Hanover County. Upon his retirement last fall, his number one deputy, Buck Lawson, had taken over as interim sheriff. And Buck, until approximately three months ago, had been my husband.

17

The downside of living in a town as small as Hansonville is that it's really hard to avoid your ex-husband, and even harder to avoid people who want to *talk* to you about your ex-husband… which wouldn't be quite so bad if they did not also want to talk about his new girlfriend. Buck and I had parted as amicably as was possible under the circumstances, but that didn't mean I was as anxious to be on the receiving end of that kind of helpful gossip as certain people were to dish it out. So I was glad that, with the holidays over and the weather turning ugly, most people were as content to stay indoors and mind their own business as I was.

The other downside of living here, especially in the winter, is that shortly after Christmas every year, without fail, the economy takes a nose dive. We call it the dead season. Retailers shorten their hours and restaurants are only open on weekends. Municipal employees take long lunches and get caught up on paperwork. Even the construction business, which had been booming all autumn due to the resort community that was being built practically in my backyard, had slowed to a crawl. About the only people who were working full time in this county were school teachers and librarians.

At Dog Daze, we are barely open at all in the winter, and this year was worse than most since we had been closed for remodeling since October. We were finally open again, but word had been a little slow to get out. So far the only dogs to enjoy the newly expanded, refurbished and freshly painted facility had been my own. Nonetheless, I opened the office every day and pretended to go to work—partly because, with its new under-floor radiant heating system, the kennel facility was actually warmer than my house, partly because I loved the smell of new paint in my brightly lit blue and yellow office, but mostly because, after being out of work for almost three months, I was *bored*.

So every morning I spent an hour or so in the indoor agility ring with my golden retriever, Cisco, working on the skills we would need when the competitive agility season began in the spring, and another half hour working with Mischief and Magic, the Aussies, in obedience. Then, because there is such a thing as over-training, I would go to my bright, clean, fresh-paint-smelling office and make busy work for myself—cutting out paper mortarboard hats for the puppy kindergarten graduates, pasting stick-on gold emblems on graduation certificates, printing out extra copies of obedience homework—while the dogs snoozed on the snuggly warm floor. Today, I had decided to update the website with photos of our brand new facility, including a happy golden retriever scrambling over the A-Frame (and totally missing his contact point, which I hoped no one would notice from the photograph) and excited Australian shepherds bounding over the broad jump with dumb bells in their mouths. I had taken the photos only that morning on the smartphone I had gotten for Christmas, which was one reason the dogs were practically comatose on the floor now. I was determined to prove that the phone was *not* smarter than I was, and it had taken quite a few tries before I had gotten a photograph that in any way resembled a dog doing anything at all. Now all I had to do was figure out how to upload those photographs to my website.

That task was proving easier said than done, which was why I was still in the office when the business line rang. The sound jarred me out of my internet-induced stupor and I jumped, banging my knee on the underside of the desk, knocking over an empty coffee cup. My dedicated canines, who had been passing the gray, dripping day as all God's creatures should—sleeping soundly in a warm, dry place—immediately sprang into action. Mischief, the Australian shepherd, ran to the window, placed her front paws on the sill, and peered out excitedly. Her sister Magic jumped up on the front door and pawed the handle, signaling that she wanted to go out. And Cisco, intrepid retriever that he was, immediately began circling the room looking for something to retrieve. He finally found one of the galoshes I had left at the door and brought it to me happily, his big plumy tail fanning an enthusiastic breeze while I pried the rubber boot from his mouth with one hand and balanced the phone against my ear with the other.

Under ordinary circumstances, I would have been glad to be distracted from my frustration by the ringing of the telephone, but I knew from experience what kind of calls I got on the office line this time of year. The Christmas puppy was relieving himself all over the house; could I tell them how to make him stop (for free)? The new dog just wasn't working out, did I know anybody who wanted him? And if not, could I keep him (for free)? Their Rottweiler/ pit bull mix, which they had never bothered to take to obedience school, had attacked the meter reader; could I help them avoid a law suit (for free?).

Consequently, my voice was a little less than chirpy as I answered the phone. "Dog Daze, this is Raine speaking."

In all the confusion of my own dogs' antics, I missed the first few words from the speaker on the other end, but perked up when I caught the last part of her inquiry. "–wondering whether you do therapy dog certification."

This sounded like someone who might actually be a paying client, so I snapped my fingers at Cisco and signaled him to sit down, then tossed the boot in the middle of the floor to get the attention of the Aussies, who took one look at my stern expression and sank guiltily to the floor. In my most professional voice I replied, "We do offer a therapy dog class here, or I'll be glad to arrange for private lessons. Has your dog had any previous obedience training?"

"Well, he's never been to a formal school," she replied cheerfully, "but he knows how to sit and come and all that. He's a very good dog."

Because I was, after all, actively soliciting new clients, I refrained from launching into a lecture about what would happen if you tried to get a child into college by claiming, "Well, he's really never been to school, but he knows how to read and write and all that." Instead, I said, "That's great, then. He shouldn't have any trouble at all finishing our basic obedience course, and then we can move him up into therapy dog training."

"Oh." She sounded disappointed. "How long will that take?"

"The basic course is eight weeks long, and the therapy dog course is six weeks."

Even before she spoke, I was waving good-bye to the cash. "Oh dear," she said. "Can't you just certify him without making him take the class?"

"I'm not actually a therapy dog evaluator," I explained to her. "I'm a trainer. I prepare you and your dog to take the certification test. The test itself is offered in Asheville several times a year."

"Asheville?" She was sounding more and more unhappy. "That's pretty far away, isn't it?"

And that was my first clue, as if I needed one, that she wasn't from around here. Asheville, which is not quite two hour's drive, is practically next door to the residents of Hanover County, who are accustomed to driving half a day to pick up a tractor part.

I said, "Well, it's really a fairly complex procedure. The evaluator has to find a facility that can simulate a medical environment, and she has to put together a team of volunteers to help with the test—"

"Medical environment? Oh, no, I don't need anything like that! I just need someone to certify my dog for therapeutic work so he can go on the wilderness retreat with me. You see, I'm a counselor with the New Day Wilderness Program, and we're allowed to take our dogs with us into the wilderness if they're certified. Something about insurance."

It was all starting to sound familiar to me now. I sat up a little straighter in my chair, raising a warning "stay" finger to both Cisco and Magic, who looked as though they were ready to claim they thought I had changed my mind about asking them to be still. Mischief yawned, stretched, and sank back down into a sphinx in the middle of the floor, pretending disinterest.

I said, "Well, there's really only one kind of therapy dog evaluation, and it involves testing the dog to make sure he's safe around children, old people, medicated people, all kinds of unexpected situations..."

"But we're not going to be around sick people or old people. We're going to be in the wilderness."

"In the middle of the winter?"

"Oh yes, we take groups out every two weeks year round."

I typed "New Day Wilderness Program" into my search engine.

"And y'all are here in Hanover County?"

"That's right. Off of Highway 81."

I scrolled through a few irrelevant listings until I found it. "New Day Wilderness Program, a therapeutic retreat for..." I clicked.

I said, "I might be able to be of more help to you if I knew what it was exactly you needed your dogs to do. Maybe the Canine Good Citizen test is all you need."

"Do you have to take a class for that?"

"It helps, but it's not necessary."

A picture came up on my browser of a peaceful-looking lodge-like retreat set amidst a stand of pines. "New Day Wilderness Program" was written above it in serene green script, and below it "Alternative therapies for the troubled teen."

"Can you give Max the test today?"

"Max?"

"My dog."

I clicked on a button at random and a montage of photographs came up—the gleaming pine interior of the lodge's dining hall, something that looked like a dormitory with neatly made bunk beds lining the walls, an outdoor shot of a suspension bridge, a rock wall, a rope swing, youthful faces illuminated by a campfire, the generic waterfalls, rushing streams and rhododendron, none of which told me any more about the place than I already knew.

I said, "It sounds as though the best thing for me to do would be to find out what kind of test your dog really needs. Maybe I should talk to the person in charge?"

She sounded relieved. "Yes, that sounds like a great idea. His name is Paul Evans." She gave me the number. "Can you call him today? We're supposed to leave this weekend, and I don't know what I'm going to do with Max if I can't take him with me."

Well, what do you know about that? I just happened to own a boarding kennel.

"Let me see what I can find out," I told her, "and I'll get back to you. But don't worry. I'm sure we'll be able to work out something for you and Max."

"Thank you," she told me sincerely. "Max means a lot to me and I don't know what I'd do if…

well, just thank you." She gave me her cell phone number and added, "You'll let me know today, right? We're allowed to take calls up until nine p.m."

"Well, well, well," I said thoughtfully to Cisco when I hung up. "It looks like we might be able to pay the dog food bill around here this month after all."

Cisco quirked his ears and tilted his head at me in a most endearing fashion, but didn't dare break his stay. I smiled approvingly at him, counted to five—because it never pays to let your dog think he's manipulated you—and said, "Okay, release!"

All three dogs bounded over to me for their obligatory ear-scratches and rib-rubs, wiggling with delight at their own magnificence. I laughed and tossed them each a treat from the canister I kept on my desk, just because they were mine and I loved them.

I turned back to the website for the New Day Wilderness Program, absently stroking Cisco's head as I began to look through it more studiously. When you're a small business owner—especially in the rural Smoky Mountains in the dead of winter with quarterly taxes hanging over your head like the Sword of Damocles—you're always on the lookout for creative ways to expand your income. (This, by the way, is the explanation for all those storefront signs you see in this part of the country that read, "Live Bait and Nutritional Supplies" and "VCR Repair and Antique Quilts" and, yes, "Attorney at Law/Taxidermist"). It occurred to me that, since two people had now called me from the same place in desperate need of my services, and since, according to the website, there were no less than six counselors on duty at one time and assuming they all had dogs… it wasn't completely beyond reason to think I might have something to offer the New Day Wilderness program that might be a little more lucrative than the $5.00 per dog test fee suggested by the AKC for the Canine Good Citizen test. At the very least, it might be worth meeting with Mr. Paul Evans to find out.

Besides, I was curious. I picked up the telephone and dialed the number of the New Day Wilderness Program's administrative offices.

I had a two o'clock appointment with Paul Evans, executive director, less than three minutes later.

CHAPTER FOUR

The headquarters of the New Day Wilderness Program was exactly as depicted on its website: a clean and modern-looking A-Frame log lodge that was nestled at the base of a mountain and whose tall glass prow looked out over serene woodland. It was three miles off Highway 81, down a wide but unpaved dirt road, and I couldn't help noticing an occasional glint of chain link fencing from the woods that lined the road on either side. Tall iron gates with the emblem of a rising sun on them were painted an attractive green, and they were open when I arrived. Closed, they would be virtually unscalable. A stand of Leland Cyprus defined the property and served as a disguise for the ten foot tall iron fence that enclosed the compound. All that was missing was the razor wire.

I had done a little more internet research and had discovered that the New Day Wilderness

Program was a therapeutic camp for troubled teens that promised parents a four-to-six-week treatment regimen that would address behavioral issues such as defiance, belligerence, moodiness, rebelliousness, lack of interest in school, secretiveness and substance abuse. Since I did not know a teenager who had not at one time or another exhibited one of those symptoms, I figured New Day must do a pretty good business. I couldn't help but notice they did not exactly promise a cure for the behaviors—at least not on their website. On there, they mainly urged anxious parents to "Call Now" and "Don't Let Another Day Go By." Of course, what I found most interesting was that they mentioned "animal therapy" as one of their tools, and even showed a picture of a young man on horseback and another of a girl hugging a yellow lab in a therapy dog vest. Paul Evans and his wife Rachel were both certified counselors, and they advertised a staff of trained therapists, social workers and wilderness experts, with a one-to-one ratio of staff to students on every wilderness expedition. It all sounded very impressive—and expensive. And now that I was here, it looked as expensive as it had sounded. I couldn't help wondering, though, given all the security I had noted as I drove up, whether all that glass on the lodge was bulletproof.

I parked in the small asphalt lot, which was discretely marked with a wooden "Visitors" sign, and walked up to the tinted-glass door. When I tried to open it, it didn't budge, and then I saw the small brass sign next to a buzzer that said "Please ring for admittance." I did, and the tinny sound of a man's voice came from the intercom at my elbow. "May I help you?"

"My name is Raine Stockton," I said. "I have an appointment with Mr. Evans."

"Oh yes, Miss Stockton. I'm glad you could make it. Come in and have a seat. I'll be with you in a minute."

I heard a lock disengage, and this time when I pushed at the door, it opened.

The interior was spacious and carpeted in soft beige, flooded with soft light from the glass apex of the building. There was a tall stone wall with a gas fire dancing in the fireplace, some leather sofas and chairs, a few end tables with neatly stacked magazines on them. I took a seat on the edge of the sofa in front of the fireplace, and while I waited, I casually glanced through a stamped leather book with the New Day rising sun logo on it. It looked like a yearbook, with big glossy pages headlined with words like "Trial" which showed kids in New Day tee shirts on the rock climbing wall and "Triumph" with photos of more New Day kids standing atop a real mountain in their climbing gear with a magnificent landscape spread out below. On another page there was a picture of a German shepherd in a therapy dog vest, and as I flipped through, I saw bright-faced young people standing beside yellow labs, black labs, golden mixes, shepherd mixes, and terrier mixes. Every good publicist knows the value of a dog picture when it comes to selling, and, so apparently, did the New Day Wilderness Program. On the very last page was a group picture of last year's counseling team, and sure enough, right in front was a blond-haired young man, kneeling with his arm around the neck of a goofy-looking black lab with a white star on his chest and a crooked right ear. The caption was "At New Day, We Care."

A man came down the corridor toward me, his hand extended. "Miss Stockton, I presume. I'm Paul Evans. Welcome to New Day."

He was a wiry man with a grey-tinged beard, slightly thinning brown hair, and unprepossessing steel-rimmed glasses. His smile was broad and his manner welcoming, and I got the impression, when he shook my hand, of strength, competence, and efficiency. He looked like the kind of man you could trust to take your troubled teenager on a wilderness expedition, which was, of course, the point.

"Thank you for seeing me," I said, glancing around. "Wow, this place is really nice. I never knew it was here."

He smiled. "There's a certain need for discretion, as I'm sure you understand. We've been here for about three years now. We just don't advertise. Come on back to my office where we can talk. The kids are in session now, so I have plenty of time."

"I looked at your website," I said, "but it didn't really give a lot of details. How many, um, residents do you have?"

"Right now we have a dozen in residence. We take them out on wilderness expeditions in groups of four to six for two weeks at a time. The rest of their time here is spent in supervised training exercises and intensive therapy to prepare them for their wilderness experience." As he spoke he led the way down a hallway that resembled the corridor of a swanky ski resort. The interior walls were formed of glossy sealed logs, the architectural ceiling beams were exposed, and the art looked to be real, not prints. "Our goal is teach cooperation, communication and confidence, and we believe the best way to do that is with the greatest teacher of all, nature."

"Sounds good to me," I murmured politely. What it sounded like was a sales pitch, but I did like the part about building confidence through communication and cooperation. That wasn't too different from my approach at Dog Daze.

He opened a door and gestured me to precede him into a nicely appointed office with a spectacular view of the Smoky Mountains through the triangular floor-to-ceiling window on the west wall. The room had its own cozy fireplace, and the credenzas and wooden filing cabinets had handles made of polished antler. On the wall behind the desk was a six-foot-tall painting of a stag on a mountaintop framed in intricately carved bark. There were two tapestry-covered wing chairs in front of the desk; the print on one was of golden retrievers in a duck blind, and on the other were black Labs in a wheat field. I had admired both chairs in a very pricey furniture shop in Asheville, but couldn't afford them.

I chose the golden retriever chair and Paul Evans sat behind the desk, his smile inviting me to state my business. So I did.

"I noticed on your website that you use therapy dogs as part of your program," I said.

"Occasionally. It's all part of the nature experience."

"Well, as I told you on the phone, I'm a dog trainer and a CGC evaluator, and I've had a couple of calls from your counselors asking me to certify their dogs as either therapy dogs or Canine Good Citizens. As I'm sure you can appreciate, that's not something I can do on twenty-four hours' notice..."

He raised a staying finger, his expression rueful. "Absolutely. I apologize if you've been bothered by the calls. Let me explain. Most of our field counselors are young people here on internships that last three to six months, and one of the most attractive things about our program is that we do allow pets in the staff dorms. However, we can only allow dogs to interact with the students if they are part of a certified therapy dog team, or at the very least have a Canine Good Citizen Certificate. Unfortunately, most of the kids don't realize that until they are assigned an expedition and only have a couple of days to make arrangements for their pets."

I nodded. "There's a huge difference between a family pet, even a well-behaved one, and a working dog team. In fact, I'm not sure I'd be entirely comfortable even taking a CGC certified dog on a wilderness expedition like the one you're describing."

A slight quirk of his eyebrow suggested I might have overstepped my bounds—particularly for someone who was about to ask for a job—but keeping my opinions to myself had never been one of my strong points. He was polite enough to inquire, "Oh?"

"For one thing," I explained, "CGC testing does not include off-leash reliability, and there are times in woods when it simply isn't practical to keep your dog leashed. My own dog, Cisco, is a canine good citizen and a certified therapy dog, but it took him over a year to get his Level One wilderness SAR certification."

He looked interested now. "You're certified for wilderness search and rescue?"

"I am," I clarified, "but Cisco is only certified for trail searches. It's a fairly complicated system, and the SAR organization I belong to has pretty high standards, but that's my point. Therapy dogs are mostly evaluated for their temperament and reliability in urban situations. A trail dog should have a little more specialized training, and so should the handler." I could see by the thoughtful look in his eye that I had made a point, so I seized my opportunity. "So, I was wondering," I plunged on, "whether you'd be interested in setting up a regular training program for your counselors and dogs. I could design it around your needs and hold the classes here if you like. As long as we have an on-going arrangement, I'm sure I could keep my prices very reasonable, and—"

There was a soft knock on the door and a woman pushed it open. "Paul," she said, barely glancing at me, "sorry to interrupt, but I thought you'd want to know Darien just got back from the doctor. It's definitely flu and there's no way she's going to be ready to go out day after tomorrow."

"Damn it," he muttered, scowling at her, "I thought these kids were supposed to have their flu shots."

She shrugged. "The doctor said sometimes they don't work."

I glanced at her, trying not to look in the least annoyed by the fact that she had interrupted just as I was winding up to my big pitch, but I might as well have been another piece of furniture. She was a plain and impossibly thin woman in her mid-forties with long, lank brown hair, weary eyes and no makeup. She wore a sweatshirt with the green rising sun of the New Day Wilderness Program logo on it, and jeans that bagged on her small frame. She stood only a few feet inside the room with her hand still on the door, as though uncertain whether to stay or go after she delivered her message.

It was at that moment that Paul seemed to remember his manners and drew himself from his frowning reverie. "I'm sorry," he said with a forced smile. "Raine Stockton, this is my wife Rachel. Rachel, Raine is a dog trainer who might be interested in working with us."

Rachel spared me a quick glance, apparently decided I wasn't worth worrying about, and turned back to Paul. "What do you want to do about the expedition? If we're going to cancel, we should do it now."

He returned sharply, "We're not going to cancel."

"But what am I supposed to—"

"I said it's under control, Rachel." This time his voice could have cut steel and I saw a dull magenta flush creep up the sallow cheeks of his spouse. Then, in a slightly milder tone he added, "I'll take care of it."

She looked at him for a moment, and if repressed emotions could ignite static air, we all would have gone up in flames. Then she nodded, turned sharply, and closed the door behind her with a definitive *snick*.

Paul Evans looked at me for half a beat when she was gone, and then said abruptly. "Miss Stockton, I'll be frank. Your coming here today was fortuitous. If you would consider joining our staff as a field specialist on a trial basis for the next week, I feel certain we could work something out regarding the training program you mentioned."

I blinked. "But—I'm not looking for a job. I have a job. Two of them, in fact. I work part time for the forest service and—"

"Forest service, really?" Again there was that spark of interest in his eyes. "Perfect. I couldn't ask for better qualifications. What I'd need for you to do is come along on our next wilderness expedition—with your therapy dog, of course—and give a few lectures on wilderness survival, maybe demo some SAR techniques... You're certified in CPR and First Aid, I assume?"

I stared at him. "Well, yes, but..."

"We leave in two days and return in ten." He slid open his desk drawer and pulled out some papers. "I'll need you to fill out some personal information and a health record on yourself and your dog. Here's an equipment list. We provide the meals and there's a lodge halfway up where you can have a hot shower, but for the most part we expect the staff to provide an example to the young people by roughing it just like they do. For someone with your experience that shouldn't be a problem, am I right?"

He was right. I had spent half my life backpacking through the Nantahala, with and without a dog. While some people might have found the prospect of sleeping in a tent in below-freezing temps, drinking hot Jell-O out of a tin cup for energy and peeing in a half-frozen stream in the middle of the night while the wind howled through the icy branches overhead a somewhat less than beguiling prospect, to me it sounded like just the kind of adventure I could sink my teeth into. My aunt and uncle had gone on a Christmas cruise, my best friend Sonny was spending the winter in a beach house on the coast, and even my business partner Maude had gone to Florida for the holidays. What had I done? Stayed at home with the dogs. Granted, a winter wilderness camping expedition was not exactly on par with sipping Mojitos in the Bahamas, but it was better than sitting around an empty office waiting for the phone to ring. For a moment I actually considered it.

But only for a moment.

I found a professional, if regretful, smile as I started to rise. "Mr. Evans, I appreciate the offer, and your confidence in me, but I'm really not looking for…"

"It pays two thousand dollars," he said.

I sat back down again.

"What trail do you take?" I asked.

"Our expedition takes place completely on private property," he said, "which we lease from Carolina Power and Electric. We hike four miles a day through moderate terrain for four days to the top of what I believe the locals call Angel Head Mountain." He smiled. "I can't tell you how it got that name. It doesn't look anything like an angel's head."

I, of course, knew exactly why the mountain was called Angel Head. It was one of the highest peaks in the region, so high that if you reached the top you could wave to the angels—so they said. It had also been the place where more than one unfortunate hiker had met his own angel over the years, and I couldn't imagine why anyone would think a winter hike to the peak of Angel Head would be fun.

Then I remembered that this particular hike was not supposed to be fun.

I said, "That's a pretty big challenge for city kids."

His expression was bland. "Challenging them is exactly what we're here to do, Miss Stockton."

I thought for a minute. "I really don't have much experience with troubled teenagers." Nor did I want to have any.

"Your role would be mostly supervisory. You wouldn't be required to participate in the therapeutic program."

Well, that was a relief, since I had no idea what the therapeutic program was.

"How many kids did you say you'd be taking out?"

"This session we're taking five. And because the remaining students will be going home tomorrow, both Rachel and I will be free to lead the expedition, along with an intern counselor, which is a one-to-two ratio." He added, "If you decide to join us, the ratio will be slightly higher."

Still, the website had promised one-to-one. I was beginning to see the problem.

I glanced down at the paperwork he had pushed in front of me. "There's no contract, right? This is just a one-time thing?"

"Absolutely. We frequently subcontract with specialists to enhance the New Day Wilderness Program. Although," he added somewhat apologetically, and with a thoroughly endearing smile, "we usually like to give them a little more notice than this."

"Tell me again what I would have to do."

"For the most part, you would be on hand to supervise procedures and answer questions from the students. Every afternoon after group therapy, we introduce an educational topic, and you would be responsible for at least three of those. Whatever you're comfortable with presenting would be fine, but I know our students would be interested in anything that has to do with dog training or search and rescue. Additionally, you and your dog would act in the role of a typical therapy dog team, as needed."

Nothing about that scenario intimidated me.

After all, I'd been teaching three-month-old puppies who didn't even speak English how to perform socially acceptable behaviors for almost ten years now; I was perfectly comfortable delivering lectures on my favorite subject to almost grown-up teenagers. I said, with only a little hesitation, "And you said it pays…?"

"Two thousand dollars for the expedition," he assured me. "Customarily, of course, our wilderness adventures last two weeks, but in the winter we've found it's more practical to keep the actual field time down to ten days."

"I can understand that," I murmured. Then, "When do you need to know?"

He smiled. "Now would be best. But tomorrow morning would be acceptable."

There was definitely nothing soft-sell about this fellow. I fingered the papers, unconsciously pulling them closer to me until I had folded them and slipped them into my purse. "I have to think about it," I said.

He passed a card to me across the desk. "Call me on my cell when you decide," he said. "Anytime tonight or in the morning. Meantime, how would you like a tour of the facility?"

He showed me a spotless dining hall, a

recreation facility with an indoor pool and basketball court, boys' and girls' dorms with military-made beds and footlockers so precisely aligned that, if you looked at them from the doorway, they formed a single unbroken line from wall to wall. There was a counseling room and a meditation room, whose doors he didn't open. We had just reached the entry lobby again, with its tall windows and dancing fire, when the front door buzzed open and a big black lab with one crooked ear and a white star on his chest bounded in. He was followed by a young woman in an anorak jacket with a leash in her hand, calling, "Max! Come back here!"

The dog ignored her and made a bee-line toward us. I did a quick pivot, showing the dog my back, and dug into my jeans' pocket for a liver treat. What kind of dog trainer would I be if I couldn't put my hands on a liver treat with one hundred percent accuracy whenever I needed one? As I expected, Max bounced off the backs of my knees and, when he was unable to get the attention wanted, immediately jumped on Paul Evans with all four paws.

The woman called, "Max, don't!"

Paul shouted, "Get down!" and shoved the dog

hard. Max, of course, thought this was a great game and bounded toward him again. This time I was ready to distract him before his paws hit the fabric, placing the treat in front of his nose and turning his head away from his target. This threw him off balance in mid-jump and he skidded into a sloppy sit. I popped the treat into his mouth with a "Good off!" just as his young owner came running up and snapped the leash to his collar.

"I'm so sorry," she gasped. "I didn't know anyone was here. Max, bad dog!"

I quickly slipped Max another treat before he started to believe he *was* a bad dog. "That's a good sit, Max," I said, but Paul Evans spoke over me.

"Heather, what are the rules about dogs on campus?"

The young woman flushed. "On leash at all times. I'm sorry, Mr. Evans."

He was still brushing imaginary paw prints from his jeans, and I could feel the anger radiating from him. So I quickly extended my hand to Heather and said pleasantly, "Hi, I'm Raine Stockton. I think we spoke on the phone."

She looked from me to her boss, trying unobtrusively to wrestle an excited Max into submission while shaking my hand. Her expression was hopeful. "Did you come to give Max his test? Will he be able to go with me this weekend?"

I privately thought the good-natured but excitable Max was at least three obedience courses away from passing his CGC test, much less a Therapy Dog evaluation, but I saw no reason to hurt her feelings. "I'm afraid not," I told her.

"Miss Stockton will be joining our staff as a field specialist." Paul recovered his composure and resumed his mild, authoritative manner. "She'll be bringing her own search and rescue dog to demonstrate survival techniques and to show us how a real working dog is supposed to behave."

I wasn't nearly as confident in Cisco's ability to demonstrate exemplary behavior as I was in his tracking skills, but I thought discretion might be the better part of valor on that topic, so I merely pulled out a business card from my pocket and handed it to a disappointed-looking Heather. Max immediately tried to eat it.

"I have a boarding kennel," I told her, "and we'd be happy to take care of Max while you're gone. You can bring him by anytime tomorrow. Just give me a call before you come for directions."

She looked at the slightly soggy business card with relief while Max danced around her feet.

"Thanks," she said. "At least I'll know he's safe."

I assured her that we provided the best care anywhere and bent down to pet the Lab's shoulder. "He's a great looking dog," I said. "How old?"

"Four," she answered immediately. "My parents gave him to me for my birthday. He's a special dog. That's why I wanted to have him with me when I took this internship."

"You're both lucky," I told her. "Not many workplaces are dog-friendly." I gave Max one last ear rub and turned to my potential new employer. "Thank you for the tour," I said.

"I look forward to working with you," he replied, taking my hand again in his firm, dry one. "And your dog, of course."

"I have some things to work out first." Like who was going to run Dog Daze now that we had an actual playing client. "I'll let you know first thing in the morning." I bent and scratched Max behind the ears. "Bye, Max. See you soon."

Heather smiled at me, and Max tried to jump up and lick my face. Heather hauled him back just in time, and I laughed. I couldn't help noticing that Paul did not, and his tone, when he spoke, was a little sharp. "If you'll excuse me, Miss Stockton, I have students to attend to and so does Miss

McBane. I look forward to hearing from you."

And just like that, he turned and walked back down the hall to his office.

Heather started to hurry away as well, but I managed to catch her eye. "Be sure to bring Max's shot records when you bring him in," I said.

She said, "No problem. I had to get everything updated before I brought him out here."

"I figured. You've been here awhile, then?"

She shook her head, flashing me a quick smile. "This will be my first trip out. I got here just after Christmas."

Now I was confused. I dropped my hand to Max's head, absently massaging his one crooked ear. "But I saw Max's picture in the yearbook." I nodded to the book on the cocktail table.

It was as though a shutter came over her eyes, and her face. "No," she said flatly, "you didn't. We just got here."

"But—"

"A lot of dogs look alike," she said firmly, tightening Max's leash. "I have to go."

I didn't often make mistakes about dogs, but I had not kept her here to talk about Max. I said quickly, "Do you mind if I ask you something?"

She pulled Max close to her and looked at me

uncertainly.

"Why would a man who doesn't like dogs want to make them a part of his therapy program?"

She wound another loop of the leash around her hand. Poor Max was standing on his tiptoes now, tongue lolling, still fantasizing that he could break away and jump up on me at any moment. Heather's lips compressed briefly. "It isn't dogs he doesn't like," she said, and there was no mistaking the note of bitterness in her voice. "It's anything—or anyone—he can't control." Alarm flashed in her eyes as she seemed to realize what she had said, and she added quickly, "What I mean is, discipline is the cornerstone of the New Day program. Structure is essential to recovery, and it's important to demonstrate that to the students in every aspect of their lives here." She tried a quick apologetic smile. "So an out-of-control dog isn't a very good role model for out-of-control teenagers."

I replied easily, "Well, I guess I can't argue with that." I tried to chat with her a little more, but she seemed nervous and anxious to get away. It could have been simply because her dog *was* out of control, and as anyone who's ever tried it knows, it's very difficult to have a normal conversation while trying to keep a seventy pound Labrador from mauling the person you're talking to.

But I thought it was more than that.

And I also thought her first answer to my question about Paul Evans was the most accurate one: he didn't like things he couldn't control, which I suppose was not an unusual characteristic for someone who ran a camp for wayward teenagers. Every now and then, I'd get a guy like that in one of my obedience classes, but he never lasted long. For one thing, those kinds of men don't have the patience to train a dog. For another, they never, ever tolerate taking orders from a woman.

If I did decide to take the job with New Day, I could tell already it would be a very interesting ten days.

CHAPTER FIVE

I was perusing the literature from the New Day Wilderness Program later that afternoon when my phone rang. I pushed a button and the rather handsome face of the person who had given me the phone for Christmas appeared. "Hi, baby," he said.

"I am not your baby," I told him and made sure to frown, even though I was happy to hear from him and I knew he had only said that to annoy me.

"Sorry, wrong number."

My relationship with Miles Young was somewhat complicated, although it had definitely been on the upswing the past few weeks. On the one hand, it was he who was responsible for the desecration of my mountain in favor of a fly-in resort community and, in principle, he represented everything I had spent my life standing against. On the other hand, well, I really liked him. And he was perhaps the main reason I didn't feel completely comfortable throwing stones at my philandering ex-husband. After all, I had moved on, too.

"Say, Miles," I said, pushing aside the New Day paperwork and turning back to my computer, "Do you know how to upload photos to a website from this phone?"

"Not a clue," he replied cheerfully. "Why don't you ask the expert?"

The picture on the screen tilted, followed by some clattering in the background, and the close-up face of Miles's nine-year-old daughter Melanie appeared. "Raine, look what Pepper can do!"

The screen tilted again and then focused on a golden retriever puppy who was holding a perfect sit and staring fixedly at the dog biscuit balanced on the end of her nose. Even as I started to cheer, I heard Melanie say, "Pepper, sit pretty." And the puppy slowly raised her front paws, balancing on her hindquarters for a good two seconds without upsetting the dog biscuit perched on her nose. Melanie declared, "Release!" just as the puppy started to wobble. The dog biscuit toppled from her nose and the puppy snatched it midair.

I laughed out loud in delight, clapping my hands wildly. Cisco, who had been snoozing by the fire, came bounding over to investigate, and the two Aussie sisters soon followed. I tried to pet them all before their happy noses and wiggling butts knocked the phone out of my hand. "Melanie, that's great!" I said. "Pepper, good girl!" I laughed again as the screen was filled with a sniffing golden retriever nose. Cisco pushed his own nose under my hand and tried to lick the phone, but I rescued it just in time.

Melanie's plump face appeared again, surrounded by a riot of dark curls and framed by black glasses. "Pretty good, huh?" She grinned proudly. "We've been practicing all week."

Less than a month ago, Pepper had been the runt of a litter of puppies that had been abandoned on my doorstep. Now she was living the good life in an Atlanta mansion with mani-pedis once a week, doggie day care and spa treatments, and a little girl who needed her even more than Pepper needed a good home. These kinds of rewards come rarely in dog rescue work, but when they do, they are worth all the sleepless nights, the mammoth dog food bills, the ruined carpets and the broken hearts that have gone before.

"Perfect," I told her. "And keep it up. Balancing exercises are great for developing strength in her spine, and she'll need that if she goes into agility.

How's she doing in puppy kindergarten?"

Melanie, who in addition to being an extremely bright child, had a natural knack for dog training and her father's tendency to become passionately dedicated to whatever interested her, began to reel off a list of Pepper's accomplishments. Naturally, she and Pepper were at the top of their class, but she was a bit worried that their instructor might not be qualified to take Pepper as far as she was capable of going. I assured her that Atlanta was filled with top dog trainers, and that when Pepper was ready to move on, I'd make sure she got into one of the best training clubs. Thus reassured, Melanie told me how to upload the photos to my website—naturally, there was an app for that—and put her father back on the phone.

"Guess what I'm going to do this weekend?" I told him, and until I said it, I didn't realize that I had already made up my mind.

"Don't even make me guess. We'll be here all night."

"Cisco and I are going on a ten-day wilderness hike with five juvenile delinquents to the top of Angel Head Mountain."

His expression remained nonplussed. "Okay. That I would not have guessed."

He was a good-looking man with short spiky salt-and-pepper hair and a firm, square jaw line. He was at his home desk with the corner of his laptop just visible and the movement of Melanie and Pepper forming shadows in the background. I could see his fingers moving on the computer keyboard as he added, "Is that one of those boot camp wilderness programs you hear about on TV?"

Clearly, I did not watch enough television. "I guess. I really hate it when you do that, you know."

"Do what?"

"Multitask."

"Sorry." A few more keystrokes, then he said, "Here it is. I thought I remembered something CNN did a few years back. Sending you the video." He closed the laptop and gave me his full attention. "So what are you and Cisco going to do on this hike across the frozen tundra?"

I made a wry face at him. "It's not the frozen tundra. It's just a few nights sleeping under the stars and eating pork and beans. It's going to be fun."

"Better you than me."

"You are pathetic."

"If you say so. I never knew there was one of those programs up there. How'd you hear about it?"

Miles had spent a lot of time and money investigating everything there was to know about this region before he had decided to invest here, and I suppose I should have been surprised that he was as unaware of New Day as I had been. Instead, I felt a little smug as I informed him, "It's called the New Day Wilderness Program. They've been here for over three years, and they lease the land for the hikes from the power company. They use therapy dogs in their program and some of the counselors called me to certify their dogs, so when I went to find out about it this guy, the director Paul Evans, offered me a job as a field specialist on their next hike."

"Smart fellow. I can't think of anyone more qualified. What exactly did you say you'll be doing again?"

"Well," I admitted, "that part I'm not too clear on, but it pays two thousand dollars."

His eyebrows went up at that. "For sleeping on the ground and eating pork and beans? Maybe you'd better read the fine print."

"As long as I don't have to be responsible for the juvenile delinquents, I don't care what the fine print says. I'm a minimum wage earner, you know."

"Well, now I feel bad. Guess where I'm going this weekend?"

"Umm… skiing in the Alps? Rafting down the Amazon?"

"Portugal."

I frowned a little. "That's in Spain, isn't it?"

"No, it's in Portugal. But you're right about one thing—it's warm and sunny there. So while you're eating frozen pork and beans, I'll be working on my tan."

"What about Melanie?"

I try not to get involved in other peoples' personal lives, I really do. Even the personal lives of people I like. I have enough trouble managing my dogs. But Miles had been a full-time father for less than three weeks, and I wondered if it might be a little soon to fall back into his cavalier globe-trotting lifestyle. Melanie had spent the majority of her life in New York with her mother—or, to be more accurate, at boarding schools with weekends in New York with her mother—who had unceremoniously abandoned custody when she decided to marry a Brazilian tennis player and live out of the country. I'm not saying Melanie had been a particular sweetheart about it in the beginning, but the fact that she had adjusted as well as she had done said a lot about her resilience. I really, really, didn't want Miles to blow it now. Because in my whole life, there have been maybe three kids that I actually have liked. Melanie is one of them. Miles said, "Grandma's coming."

And in the background, Melanie echoed, "Grandma's coming!"

Well, that was good. I hadn't actually thought he'd just leave the country and forget about her, the way a person might forget to feed the goldfish when he went away for a long weekend. But it wasn't just Melanie, now. He had a whole family to worry about, and, after all, Melanie was practically old enough to take care of herself, but Pepper was just a puppy. "Are you sure that's a good idea, Miles?" I lowered my voice a little, hoping not to be overheard by the young lady on the other end. "I mean, a puppy is a big responsibility. Does your mother even like dogs?"

For a moment his eyes were blank, and then he realized I was not talking about his daughter. The amusement that twitched his lips was rueful. "My mother was the first adult human Pepper met after you, remember? And she allowed a puppy to pee all over her sisal rugs at the beach house over

Christmas, so I think she'll be fine here. Besides, Melanie has your number."

"But I'll be in the wilderness." I was starting to wonder if I should reconsider.

"That phone will work from Mars. That's why I gave it to you. Just make sure it's charged before you leave. And, Raine." He looked for a moment as though he was going to say something stupid and patronizing like *Be careful* or, worse, *Don't go hiking up a mountain in the middle of the winter for ten days with a bunch of jailbirds you don't know*. I could see it in his eyes, and I appreciated the sentiment, but no one who knew me would have said it out loud. So he only said, "Stay warm. I'll call you from the airport."

"Have a good time. Tell Melanie I'll check on her before I leave."

It was only after I hung up that I realized, with a silly kind of wistfulness, that I really kind of wished he had said something stupid.

~

I had known Maude for most of my life. She had taught me everything I knew about dogs. It had been she who had given me my first golden retriever, and she'd been my partner in Dog Daze for fifteen years. Maude and I were accustomed to taking over for each other when we had to, and even though she had only been back from Florida a few days herself, Maude had no problem moving in with her two dogs for a week to run the kennel and take care of Mischief and Magic while I was gone. In fact, I think she was as bored as I was with the extended holiday, and she was glad to have easy access to the training facility, which would give her goldens a head start on the competitive season. She was not, however, quite as enthusiastic about the details of the expedition. "No offense intended, my dear, but young people are hardly your specialty. Haven't you told me over and over you'd rather have dinner with a golden retriever than a child any day? Why would you willingly agree to take an entire bevy of them on a wilderness hike?"

I felt compelled to defend myself. "Well, I did okay with Melanie, didn't I? She wasn't exactly a little cupcake when I first met her." She had, in fact, been a holy terror, and if the truth were told, it had been my dogs, not I, who had turned her around. Now Melanie was one of my favorite people, and the experience had suggested that there might, in fact, be other children in the world I could learn to like. "Besides," I added, "these are teenagers, not children, and I'm just going along as a field specialist." Whatever that was.

"Troubled teenagers. What kind of trouble, do you suppose?"

"Well, I don't think any of them have served time. According to the website, rebelliousness, anger, disrespect, the usual."

"Hmm. Sounds a good deal like you when you were a teenager. Perhaps you'll be of use after all."

"Thanks a lot."

Maude had clerked for my father, a district court judge, until his retirement, and had been practically a member of the family for as long as I could remember. She had pulled me out of more than one scrape as a teenager, and if she hadn't, I doubt I would've grown up to be the respectable citizen I am today. "Anyway, that only goes to prove there's hope for anyone."

"True enough. You've checked this fellow out, I suppose?"

"Sure." I guiltily remembered the video Miles had sent me, which I had not had time to watch. "That is, I'll give Buck a call in a minute, but you don't get the money for a building like that one unless you're legitimate."

"I'm certain you know what you're doing, my dear. What time shall I report for duty?"

I arranged for her to mind the kennel while I ran errands the next day, and as soon as we hung up, I dialed the sheriff's office. I was both surprised and oddly relieved when the dispatcher informed me that Buck was on vacation. In all the time we'd been married, the only vacation time Buck had taken was a few days here and there to go fishing. Of course, he hadn't been sheriff then.

And he hadn't had a cute new girlfriend to go on vacation with.

"You know things are dead around here this time of year," she went on, "and I hear the weather is great in Florida. He'll be back next week though if you want him to call you."

Florida? The farthest he had ever taken me was to the next county for a movie on Saturday night. And he hadn't even told me he was leaving. The two of us might be estranged, but we did still talk.

I guess things had really changed.

I said, "No, umm, that's okay. I just called to ask someone to check on something for me." I explained to her about New Day, and she volunteered to do a computer search while I waited on the phone. A few minutes later, she came back with a clean report: permits and licenses in order, no complaints.

"Oh, wait a minute," she said, just as I thanked her absently and was about to hang up. "Here's something. APB on a missing person last year from Bullard County, some kid went off a hiking trail. But he must've turned up because they closed out the case a couple of days later."

"Okay, sounds good, then," I told her. "Thanks for your help." And I hung up, still thinking about Buck in Florida.

And Miles in Portugal.

I called Paul Evans and took the job. He was delighted. "Report here Saturday morning at seven," he told me. "We'll provide your backpack, tent, sleeping bag, food and other supplies, and you have the list of personal items you should bring."

"I'll bring my own provisions," I assured him. Packing a backpack for a wilderness expedition was, in my opinion, like packing your own parachute. If you left the chore to someone else, you had no one but yourself to blame when things went wrong.

"That's really not necessary—"

"Thanks, but I prefer it. Besides, I have to pack for Cisco, too." Cisco was trained for backpacking and could carry most of his own food and water, but that was certainly not something I would trust to anyone but myself. "What kind of fresh water sources can we expect?"

Most people think that the cold is the biggest danger of winter camping, but it's actually dehydration. A smart camper always carries plenty of water purification tablets and makes sure his route takes him close to fast-moving streams that are unlikely to freeze.

He chuckled a little. "Plenty of fresh water, Miss Stockton. We have done this before."

I assumed that meant they would have jugs of purified water stashed along the route for the city kids. I'd bring my own water purification kit anyway.

We talked for a few more minutes about some of the demos I had planned, and he was enthusiastic. When I hung up I was feeling quite pleased with myself. Who needed Florida? Or Portugal, for that matter. I was going to have a *real* adventure.

~

I got up early the next morning and drove to Asheville for the supplies I needed: protein bars for both Cisco and me, freeze-dried dog food in pre-measured pouches that were both lightweight and nutritionally balanced, and MREs that actually tasted like the food they were purported to be. I kept most of those things on hand, but when Cisco and I went into the wilderness it was rarely for more than a day or two and I was not accustomed to supplying for over a week. I also bought Cisco a set of protective rubber booties, because you can never tell how the weather is going to turn above 3500 feet, and nothing will slow a dog down faster, or make him more miserable, than ice between his paw pads. I had a perfectly good camp stove, collapsible cup, water pouch and sleeping bag, but I spent more time than I should have in the camping store, marveling over the high- and low-tech equipment that was guaranteed to make the great outdoors as comfortable as your own living room. In the end I bought a new set of wicking long underwear, some extra wool socks—because you can never have too many pairs of dry socks—and a couple of extra lightweight heat packs. I could have spent my entire paycheck in the camping store, but made myself leave before temptation got the better of me.

The night before, I had watched the four-minute news clip Miles had sent me about wilderness rehabilitation programs for troubled teens, which were, as I suppose anyone with a troubled teen would know, fairly prevalent across the country. The programs lasted anywhere from six weeks to six months and centered around a holistic approach to wellness and recovery. In addition to psychological counseling and team-building exercises, the teens spent weeks learning wilderness survival skills and practicing them on day hikes in a relatively safe environment. Toward the end of the program, their skills were tested in the wilderness on a hike of one or two weeks' duration. Graduates of the program were said to have a 50% less likely chance for recidivism than those who attended traditional rehabilitation therapy, and in the past ten years, only one provider had fallen under scrutiny when charges of child abuse were brought—charges that were, according to the report, eventually dropped.

While I was waiting at the drive-through for a burger and fries for the trip home (after all, winter hiking uses an enormous amount of calories and I figured I could afford to bulk up), I got a text from

Miles. Personally, I think we are both too old to be texting and that was only one of the things about the new phone that I disliked. But over the past few weeks I had gradually gotten used to it.

What are you doing in Asheville?

The phone's GPS system, which was supposed to be an important safety feature, was another thing I could have lived without. You were supposed to be able to disable it, but I had not yet taken the time to discover how.

I texted back: *Are you stalking me?*

Trying to.

Where are you?

Airport. Check photos.

I pushed the icon for new photos and a picture came up of a golden retriever puppy curled up asleep atop a pile of neatly folded clothes in an open suitcase. I grinned in spite of myself.

Cute.

Boarding. Bye.

My order arrived and I received the steaming, fragrant bag with one hand while I typed with the other: *Me too. Bye.*

Actually, I was getting pretty good at this.

~

By the time I got home, Max was already comfortably installed in his private kennel, with its radiantly heated floor, elevated bed and automatic water supply, munching on a bone and surrounded by an array of toys that Heather had left for him. It occurred to me that Max, by being unqualified to go on this trip, might actually had gotten the better end of the deal.

Maude agreed with me. "His owner seemed to be a pleasant enough young lady, but I explained to her he is a good obedience course or two away from being certified for anything, much less a wilderness trail. But of course at his age, a certain lack of impulse control is only to be expected."

I was confused. "Heather told me he was four." But now that I thought of it, he did look—and act—much younger.

"Not according to his vet records. The Town and Country Animal Hospital of Pendleton, Ohio, seems to think he turned two last September, and I'm inclined to trust them, since their shot records go back to his first puppy shots at age eight weeks. Of course, she is his second owner, so perhaps she was misinformed."

I looked up from the vet record she had handed

me, frowning. "That's odd," I said. "She told me she'd had him since he was a puppy. I wonder why she would lie."

Maude gave a philosophic shrug as she returned the papers to their file folder. "I should imagine that, with ten days in the wilderness together, you'll have plenty of opportunity to find out."

But by the time I saw Heather again, a minor prevarication about her dog was the least of my concerns.

CHAPTER SIX

There is something exciting about getting up before dawn on a below-freezing morning, grabbing a cup of coffee and a bowl of instant oatmeal, and packing the car for a trip by the lights from the windows with your boots crunching on ice mud and your breath frosting the air. For Cisco and me, such mornings usually mean a competition, a tracking class, or—even better—doing what we were trained to do: a wilderness search for someone who was in trouble. Cisco's spirits were as high as mine as I hurried through my morning chores—feeding the dogs and turning them out into the exercise yard, scooping the poop, refilling water dishes, setting the thermostat, and checking my backpack and Cisco's one last time. Cisco gulped his breakfast, looking up several times to make sure I wasn't going to leave without him, raced outside for his morning toilet, and then padded through the house at my side, panting excitedly, up and down the stairs, back and forth from door to hall, as anxious to get on with the adventure as I was.

Maude was coming at nine, so I put Mischief and Magic in one of the big kennel runs next to Max, turned the lights down low, and left them with some peanut butter-smeared chew bones and classical music to pass the time. Inside the house I made sure the coffee pot was off, washed all the dog dishes and put them away, double-checked the thermostat and turned off the upstairs lights. My backpack and Cisco's were waiting beside the front door. I pulled on my hiking coat—an insulated all-weather job with zippered underarms for ventilation, elastic wrist and neck bands lined with sweat-absorbing, wind-chasing crew knit, and double fasteners to keep out precipitation—and hoisted both backpacks. "Okay, boy," I said, "let's hit the road."

Cisco turned and scampered up the stairs. "Hey!" I exclaimed. But he returned a moment later, bounding down the stairs with his favorite stuffed rabbit in his mouth. I couldn't help laughing, and after a moment's consideration, stuffed it into his backpack. After all, it couldn't weigh more than a few ounces, and even dogs need a little something to remind them of home on a long trip.

I was backing out of the driveway when I remembered my phone, which I had faithfully placed in the charger on my nightstand overnight, and where it still remained. I almost kept going. There was something about the whole concept of such a high-tech device on a pristine winter wilderness hike that jarred my sensibilities, and I thought I would be happier without it. But of course it was a survival tool, and I couldn't forget about Melanie, with whom I had promised to keep in touch, or Miles, who had accused me before of being selfish and irresponsible, not that I cared what he thought when he was in a demanding mood. Reluctantly, I put the car in gear and raced back inside for the phone.

Three minutes later, phone safely zipped in the pocket of my coat, we were off.

~

The sky was barely turning gray when I parked in front of the New Day Lodge at 6:45, but a few young people wearing backpacks and stocking caps were already milling around a green bus with the New Day logo on the side. I recognized Heather and waved to her as I got out. She half-lifted a timid, gloved hand in reply.

I got Cisco suited up in his backpack before I allowed him out of the car, and he was practically dancing with excitement before I was finished. I clipped on his hiking leash, which was constructed of a bungee-type material that expanded and contracted with his movements, and secured the other end to a carabineer on my belt before I allowed him out of the back of the SUV. He leapt nimbly to the ground, and I adjusted the weight of the saddlebags to rest equally between his shoulder blades.

"Hey, cool," I heard one of the kids say. "It's a backpacking dog!"

Cisco grinned and pricked up his ears, anxious to meet and greet, but I held up a staying finger. "Wait," I cautioned.

I slipped the straps of my own backpack over my shoulders, pressed the button on the remote control to lock the car, and started up the walk to the lodge. I spoke quietly under my breath to keep Cisco at heel, but he was so excited he was practically prancing with the effort to slow his pace to mine. I knew the kind of self-control it took for

Cisco to restrain himself from bounding forward to meet his new soon-to-be best friends, so I kept my hand free and ready to grab the leash close to his collar if or when his lesser nature got the better of him. I was, however, careful not to actually grip the leash. For one thing, I was distinctly aware that I—and my famous Search and Rescue dog—were making our first impression, and I was vain enough to want us to look like pros, even if the only people watching weren't exactly dog show judges. Secondly, most people don't realize that a tight grip on the leash only encourages a dog to pull. The last thing I needed was to start my first day as a so-called field specialist by stumbling onto the scene at the wrong end of the leash behind a galloping golden retriever.

The kids were calling, "Here, poochie, poochie!" and making cooing, "What a cute puppy!" noises from the time we left the car. Some of the little monsters were even bending forward and slapping their thighs in an almost irresistible come-hither motion, even though they could clearly see Cisco was leashed to me. My good dog, though it strained every instinct he possessed, remained more or less at my side, casting me quick eager looks every other step or so. I stopped about three feet from the crowd and put him in a sit, but that did not protect him from being mobbed by the teenagers.

Two girls rushed forward and started cooing and clucking over him, rubbing his face and practically shoving their noses against his. You'd think almost-grown-up people would know better, but I've seen adults do even stupider things with strange dogs. One of the boys pounded Cisco's ribs in what I supposed was meant to be a friendly gesture and said, "What'd ya say, old boy? What did you do to end up in a place like this?"

Another boy, a tall fellow with a lanky build, buzz-cut hair and hands stuffed into the pockets of his eight-hundred dollar, state-of-the-art, four season hiking coat (I knew because I had admired it at the sporting goods store in Asheville) drawled, "Must've pissed on a policeman's shoe to get a sentence like this."

The girls giggled, and thus encouraged, he added, "Or maybe pooped in the mayor's bed."

I said pleasantly. "Cisco has done a lot of work for the police department, and he has never peed or pooped on anyone. What about you?"

The girls really laughed at that, and so did the other boy, who added, "She got you there, Jess!"

Jess turned a dull red and scowled at them, and I felt a little bad. But, as I've said, kids are not my strong suit.

Heather came up to us. "Hi," she said. "I see you've met Jess and Pete. This is Tiffanie." A girl with a braided pigtail hat and platinum bangs looked up from petting Cisco. "And Angel." The other girl had already grown bored, and she wandered away when Heather spoke her name without acknowledging either of us. Heather gave a small half-shrug of apology and smiled at Cisco. "Your dog is gorgeous."

Heather did not look much older than her charges this morning with her face scrubbed clean and her blond hair braided down her back, but I supposed that was the point. I said, "Max is doing great. He had a big breakfast this morning and romped with my dogs for half an hour."

She looked relieved. "The woman who checked him in said she'd take him out to play every two hours. He loves to play. "

"Most Labradors do," I agreed.

I released Cisco from his sit just as a disgruntled-looking young woman pushed through the door of the lodge, hoisting her backpack. She was moderately obese with jet-black hair that was blunt-cut at her collarbone, and an unfortunate pentagram tattoo over one eyebrow. Her gait was awkward beneath the weight of her pack, and I worried about her on the hike. Cisco perked up his ears in his usual friendly fashion, and she scowled even deeper when she noticed him.

"That's Lourdes," Heather said. "The kids call her Lard-Ass. She is not," she added with a faint note of dryness in her voice, "one of our happiest campers."

Lourdes pushed by the others and jerked on the door of the bus. Finding it locked, she stomped away, shrugged out of her backpack, and sat on it.

"Yo, Lourdes," jeered the boy called Jess, "I'd be careful if I was you. You're going to turn all that trail mix into kitty litter."

Lourdes glared at him, folded her arms, and deliberately shifted her weight back and forth on the pack, making a crinkling and crunching noise that I could hear even from where I was standing.

"Lourdes, get up!" A sharp voice spoke from the steps of the lodge and we all turned as Rachel Evans came down them. She was dressed in good, all-weather hiking pants, well-worn boots, and a coat that swam on her slight frame. Nonetheless, she carried a backpack by its straps on one shoulder that looked heavy enough to unbalance a man twice her size. She said, "Your life may well depend on what's in that pack. Treat it with respect. All of you." She turned to the group at large as Lourdes reluctantly shuffled to her feet. "This is not a joke. How many times do we have to go over it? There are no second chances out here. Daddy is not going to come get you. You are responsible for your own survival, do you understand that? Do you?"

I had to admire her speech and was glad to see it had gotten their attention. In my opinion, there were too many Americans who came into the wilderness thinking it was run by the same people who managed theme parks, and by the time they discovered the animals were real and there was no fresh-faced hostess in khakis around the next corner to show them to the comfort station, it was generally too late. My job would have been a lot easier, and most of the outcomes a lot happier, if Rachel Evans had given that same speech to everyone who put on a backpack.

There was an unhappy grumble of "Yes ma'ams and "Yeah, rights," but the two boys were nudging each other and grinning, and I thought I heard one of them mutter something about a "lard-ass" under his breath.

Rachel Evans walked up to them and stood with feet apart. "Mr. Nesbit, Mr. Randall," she said, "kindly remove your backpacks and spread the contents out here on the walkway. I want to spot check your inventory."

Jess stared at her. "Are you kidding? It'll take me half an hour to repack this thing!"

"Then I suggest you hurry," Rachel replied calmly as she turned away, "because we're leaving in ten minutes."

The boys wasted one more second in incredulity, and then, with a flash of panic in their eyes, they stripped off their packs and began rapidly unloading the contents. Apparently, they had learned from experience what happened when they did not take Rachel seriously.

Rachel seemed to notice Cisco and me for the first time, and she came toward us with a small frown. "You're the new girl, aren't you?"

"I'm Raine Stockton," I reminded her. I wasn't quite sure how I felt about being called a "girl". I produced the packet of completed paperwork from my jacket pocket and handed it to her. "And this is Cisco."

She opened the papers and glanced over them, then stuffed them in a zippered outer packet of her pack. She ran her gaze over me once from head to toe, and I got the impression she wasn't very impressed. "You've been briefed on procedure?"

"Not really," I admitted. "This was pretty last-minute."

She looked annoyed. "Don't interfere with our treatment program," she said. "Exercise normal trail safety behavior. Don't socialize with the students. And keep your dog under control."

Before I could draw breath for a reply that would have been as chilly as the morning dawn, she turned and called, "Five minutes!"

The girls lined up in front of the bus doors and the boys stood beside the contents of their packs, looking impatient and a little scared. I glanced at Heather and murmured, "Charming, isn't she?"

Heather just returned a weak smile and hurried to join the girls at the bus.

Dogs are very sensitive to emotional energy, which is why a nervous handler can keep a championship dog from even making the first cut at a dog show, and why more dogs fail the long stay at an obedience trial than any other exercise. The more you think, *don't move, don't move,* the more anxious your dog is likely to become, until eventually he just has to trot over and see if you're all right. This is why it is so important for a good handler to keep her emotions neutral in all circumstances, and over the years shifting into calm mode in stressful situations had become second nature to me. I knew without even glancing at him that the unpleasant Rachel, the chattering girls and the belligerent boys were making Cisco anxious. I held out my arm, which gave him permission to jump up for a hug, and as he did, something fell out of his backpack and thudded on the ground.

Paul Evans came out of the lodge just as I lowered Cisco lightly to all four feet and bent to pick up the object that had tumbled from the pocket of his backpack. Both he and Rachel watched as I picked up the flat bottle of bourbon and stared at in puzzlement. Rachel came over to me and snatched the bottle out of my hand. "I don't believe this." Her voice was cold with fury. "You *do* know where you are, don't you? Did you even bother to read our literature?"

Paul said in a quick, calm voice, "I'm sure there's just been a mistake."

I dragged my incredulous gaze away from Rachel. "I'll say there has. That bottle is glass. If we had been standing on concrete instead of dirt when it fell, it would have broken and Cisco could have been hurt." I bent to refasten the buckle of his pack, which had, of course, been securely fastened when I put the pack on him. "Someone obviously slipped that in Cisco's pack as a joke."

Rachel's eyes blazed. "We do not consider this kind of contraband something to joke about, Miss Stockton. Some of these kids are recovering from substance abuse. We can't afford—"

"Look," I said impatiently, "I don't even like bourbon, and even if I did, the last thing I'd do is bring it along on a trip like this. Alcohol and wilderness camping don't mix, especially in the cold, when it's hard enough for a sober person to keep his body temperature up. Isn't that the kind of expertise you hired me for?"

Our little exchange was beginning to attract attention, and Paul said quietly, "Clearly, there's been a breach in our security. I suspect that one of the boys panicked when you decided to inspect their packs and tried to hide the bottle in the closest place. However, we're not going to be able to prove anything now, so why don't you just dispose of the evidence and let's get going."

She glared at me for another moment and then

stalked away.

Paul gave me an apologetic smile. "I'm sorry," he said, "This work has its own unique challenges."

I said, "I don't think it was one of the boys." I glanced at them, but they seemed far more concerned about getting back in line with the others than with what was happening with Cisco and me. "They didn't have time."

His smile this time seemed a little condescending. "Some of these young people are very devious and highly motivated. You'll learn it never pays to underestimate them. Now then." He rubbed his hands together in an unconscious washing motion, as though to rid himself of the entire unpleasant episode. "Allow me to welcome you aboard." He glanced at Cisco. "And this must be the renowned—I'm sorry, what's your dog's name again?"

"Cisco," I supplied.

"Excellent." As he spoke, his eyes swept the surroundings, counting students, checking details. "The bus will take us to the trail head, about five miles north. I'll explain a bit more about procedure on the way. Basically, we hike four to six miles daily with a skills-building exercise in the middle of each day. The students must be responsible for themselves and their own well-being, and the staff should intervene only in a case of life or death. They will set up their own tents, dig their own fire pits, cook their own food. You are here in an educational capacity only."

Just as I drew a breath to inquire what, exactly, about a winter wilderness hike would *not* be considered life or death, he turned to the group and called, "Ladies and gentlemen, your attention please."

The boys looked up anxiously from the inventory of their belongings, and the girls, looking cold and miserable, turned to him. "This is Raine Stockton," he said, "a wilderness survival specialist, and her search and rescue dog…"

He looked questioningly at me and I supplied again, "Cisco."

"Right. Ms. Stockton will be delivering several lectures and demonstrations about the wilderness experience during the course of our expedition and will be on hand to answer questions and supervise your progress. Ms. Stockton." He surprised me by turning to me and inviting, "Perhaps you'd like to share a few wilderness survival tips before we start out?"

There were, of course, a lot of helpful things I

could have said... if only I'd had an hour or two to prepare. As it was, with a half dozen pair of skeptical eyes turned in my direction, I decided to take a page from Rachel's book, in which brevity was a virtue. I met the gaze of each onlooker with calm certainty, because as any dog knows, it's important to show confidence when you find yourself in a position of leadership. I rested my hand lightly on Cisco's head and I said simply, "Don't feed my dog. Don't tease my dog. Double-knot your bootlaces and keep your socks dry. You'll be fine."

There was a beat of silence in which I could sense Paul staring at me, waiting for me to go on. When I did not, he rubbed his hands together again and declared heartily. "Well, then. Let's get underway."

~

The boys were still stuffing socks and underwear back into their packs when Paul cranked the engine of the bus, and they barely made it onboard before the doors closed. The twenty minute drive over bumpy roads was made even more excruciating by Rachel's lecture on standard-trail procedure. There was nothing wrong with her facts; it was simply that they were delivered like a drill sergeant's orientation to new recruits. I tuned her out and, with Cisco panting happily on the seat next to me, I took out my phone and texted Melanie. It was Saturday, and only a few minutes past seven a.m., but I knew she would be up. Anyone with a new puppy would be.

I'm off to the wilderness. Everything ok with you?

In a moment she typed back, *Teaching Pepper to speak today.*

Follow Me is more important.

"Follow me" was what we called puppy heeling at Dog Daze and was the first step toward teaching a dog to walk reliably at his owner's side both on and off leash. In class we practiced to music, and played "musical sits" by seeing which puppy could sit the fastest when the music stopped.

She already knows that.

She wouldn't *really* know it for at least another year, possibly two, but Melanie got her stubbornness from her father and I knew when to pick my battles. *Send me a video.*

OK. Grandma's taking me to the Pancake House for

breakfast. Bye.

I was scrolling down to check my messages when someone tapped my shoulder from behind. "We're not allowed to have phones," Heather whispered, leaning close.

I twisted around in my seat to look at her. "I'm staff," I reminded her.

She shook her head. "Doesn't matter. It's a rule."

I drew my brows together in cautious incredulity. "That's crazy."

She shrugged.

"We're going on a dangerous hike. What if there's an emergency?"

"I think Paul has a phone in his pack."

I was willing to bet that whatever phone Paul had wasn't as reliable as mine. I started to turn around again. "Luckily, so do I."

"Just don't let Rachel see it," Heather said. "She'll confiscate it."

I smothered a chuckle. As ambivalent as I had previously been about the phone, I was now quite determined that the only way anyone would get it away from me would be to pry it from my cold dead fingers. "I'd like to see her try," I said.

Nonetheless, as the bus made a turn and began

to slow to a bouncing stop and Rachel turned to face our direction, I discretely turned the phone off and returned it to my backpack.

"The first thing you will do when you leave the bus," Rachel announced clearly, "is elect a hike leader for the day."

"I nominate the pooch," one of the boys called out, and there was a lot of giggling and a few catcalls that made Cisco's ears prick forward.

"The leader will not be a member of the staff," Rachel went on as though she had not been interrupted. "He or she will be responsible for the safe and timely arrival of every member of the expedition to our night camp site, five miles up the mountain. The leader will coordinate setting up the camp, preparing the evening meal, and making certain everyone is properly provisioned for the next day's journey. He or she will designate tasks and keep his or her group on course. Your leader will make decisions that directly affect your welfare, ladies and gentlemen, so choose carefully."

"I nominate my man Jess," Pete called out.

"I nominate Lard-Ass," one of the girls added, and her seat companion grinned and elbowed her in the ribs.

"That will be one demerit, Miss Caruthers,"

Rachel said, and the girl who'd made the unfortunate "lard-ass" remark quickly lost her smile. "Our nominees are Lourdes Montego and Jess Nesbit." Rachel distributed papers and pencils to each of the kids as the bus came to a halt in the cleared area beneath a high-voltage tower. I studied the terrain and was able to discern a faint foot trail snaking off to the west. "Write down your preference and pass it to me as you exit the bus."

To no one's surprise, Jess was elected leader four to one, with the one vote for Lourdes, presumably, having been cast by herself. Grinning and posturing, Jess drew himself up and declared, "I'd like to thank the Academy, my loyal fans, and that sorry excuse for a father who banished me to this pimple on the flabby white butt of the world and made all of this…" He gestured broadly to the desolate landscape surrounding. "Possible. I promise to be a wise and benevolent ruler. I promise a chicken in every pot… or is that pot in every chicken… or is that pot in every backpack…"

By this time the kids were hysterical with laughter, and even I was having a hard time repressing a grin. I pretended to check the straps of Cisco's backpack so no one could see. I used to hang out with kids like Jess in high school, and they were never as much trouble as they liked to pretend they were. Some of them grew up to be pretty good guys.

Some of them ended up in jail.

Paul Evans hoisted his backpack, fastened the straps, and said to Jess, "I hope you know how to read a trail map and a compass, young man, because if we don't reach the first campsite by dark, your loyal fans will be sleeping in the dirt, and I doubt you'll be quite so popular in the morning."

Jess gave a cavalier shrug and replied, "How hard can it be? It's walking." He lifted his arm over his head and called, "Onward, peasants!"

And after a start like that, where could the day go but down?

CHAPTER SEVEN

The trail started out on an easy slope, and with the rising sun at our backs, the exercise was just enough to take the edge off the cold. At first, the kids bunched up together in a fairly predictable manner with the two boys in front, joking and fooling around, Tiffanie and Angel in the middle, complaining about the boys, and Lourdes trailing sullenly behind. Paul walked with Cisco and me for the first hour or so, filling me in on procedure and the day's curriculum, which really was just an elaboration on what Rachel had told me: do my job and stay out of the way while they did theirs. He just had a more personable way of explaining it.

"Today is about teamwork and cooperation," he said, "and they'll need it all to get to the camp site on time. At the end of the day the team leaders will evaluate everyone's performance on both a personal and a group basis, and you will weigh in on survival techniques—how any mistakes they made today might have been corrected, what they can do to avoid similar problems in the future, that kind of thing. Remember to keep it instructional. Our purpose is to give them tools they can use to make tomorrow's journey more profitable. That's the whole philosophy behind New Day—looking toward tomorrow."

"Sounds good to me. But I don't imagine I'll have too much to say about what went wrong." He shot me a questioning look and I explained, "If you make a mistake out here, you're going to know it. The best plan is not to make any mistakes at all."

"That may be," he agreed, "but just remember, the only way these kids learn is by making mistakes. We don't interfere."

I was not entirely sure about that. At Dog Daze, our philosophy was to set them up for success. Sure, if a dog made the wrong choice, he would suffer the consequence of *not* getting a tasty treat. But we believe that learning comes through success, not failure, so we do everything possible to make sure the dog gets more rewards than not. Of course, I did allow for the very slim possibility that what worked with dogs might not work with teenage humans, so I said nothing. After all, my degree was in wildlife biology. Paul was the accredited crisis intervention counselor, whatever that was.

We decided I would deliver a lecture on wilderness search and rescue on day three and provide a demonstration on day six. Day five, the midway point, was when we were expected to reach the camp lodge, which was kept stocked with emergency supplies and a battery-operated two-way radio. There the kids would be rewarded with a chance to shower, a meal that was not freeze-dried, and an opportunity to refill their water supplies from a source that had already been purified. He told me that the power company had set up the lodge—which was really little more than an open-air pavilion with electricity for line workers— and New Day kept it operational year round. In the summer a specialist in art and music therapy would be brought in and the group would spend a day or two there, but this time of year its use was strictly pragmatic.

"We like to stagger the positions of the staff members while hiking," he added. "You won't always be able to keep everyone in sight, particularly as the trail gets more rugged, but make certain you always know the position of the child in front of you and the child behind you. One staff member always brings up the rear, but we rotate that position during the course of the day to allow for everyone's individual pace. Any questions?"

"I'll need a trail map," I told him.

He looked at me blankly.

"A trail map," I repeated, thinking he hadn't heard. "No one gave me one this morning."

He frowned a little. "Oh, well. I'll have to check when we stop and see if I have an extra one."

He excused himself and increased his pace, leaving me in the middle of the pack between Angel and Tiffanie, with Heather bringing up the rear behind Lourdes. The boys were striding briskly along in the front, talking about cars.

I stepped off the trail to allow Cisco to relieve himself, and splashed water into his collapsible canvas bowl. Heather paused beside us as Cisco was lapping up the last of the water, and he looked up at her with a friendly wag of his tail. She obliged him by petting his head. "Good luck getting that map," she said. "I overheard you talking. He only has one, and that goes to the day leader."

Once again, incredulity crossed my eyes. "Every hiker should have a trail map," I said.

"What if we get separated? What if someone gets lost?"

She shrugged. "That's the point. Don't."

I said, "Did you hear what happened this morning? Somebody put a bottle of booze in Cisco's backpack."

Heather seemed unsurprised. "That sounds like something Jess would do. I don't know how he would have gotten his hands on alcohol, though. We're pretty much on lockdown from the time the kids enter the program until they do the hike."

"It wasn't Jess. He was nowhere near Cisco, and I was watching the other boy, Pete, the whole time he was petting him."

She said, "It might have been Rachel."

I stared at her.

"I heard her arguing with Mr. Evans about hiring you," she said. "She has kind of a reputation for being jealous of female staff members. Maybe she thought she could get you fired before you even started."

"Terrific," I muttered. It was never a good sign to start a new job by being hated by the boss's wife.

She gave me a sympathetic shrug and moved on ahead, leaving Cisco and me to take up the rear position with Lourdes.

I felt sorry for the overweight girl whose cheeks were already stained strawberry with exertion, and I tried to make conversation. "Hi, I'm Raine," I said.

She trudged on, head down, mouth sullen. "You're not supposed to talk to me."

"Sorry, I'm new," I replied easily. If she thought being rude would discourage me, she was very much mistaken. "What about you?"

She scowled at me, and then hitched up her shoulder straps. "What kind of dog is that?"

"Golden retriever. Do you have a dog?"

She grunted. "Where I come from, we put dog meat in our stew."

I lifted an eyebrow. "Good to know. Remind me never to have dinner at your house. Where do you come from?"

"You ever hear of a barrio?"

"Sure. I saw *West Side Story*."

The uneasy, slightly challenging way her eyes slid toward me from beneath her tattooed brow assured me that she had not.

"A barrio is a like a ghetto," I explained to her, "only Spanish-speaking people live there."

"Well, that's where I'm from. We cut people just for fun. On the street where I live, even the cops are afraid to come."

I shrugged. "Wherever you're from is home, I guess."

Once again she slid me an uncertain look. And since, had I been a betting woman, I would have placed money on the fact that she did *not* come from a barrio, I added, "So who did you cut to get sent here?"

"You're not allowed to ask me that."

"Sorry."

She was starting to breathe hard, so I said, "Do you want to stop and have some water?"

She said, stomping determinedly ahead, "Shut up. I could cut you."

I replied mildly, "Pretty sure you're not allowed to talk to me like that."

"Yeah, well, turn me in, bitch."

Good thing I'm a dog trainer, and know all about staying calm around out-of-control animals. I replied with a thin smile, "I know you're not allowed to talk to me like *that*."

"Miss Stockton!"

I looked up to see Rachel striding back down the trail toward me. "You've been asked not to socialize with the students."

"No problem." I clucked my tongue to Cisco

and increased my pace, leaving Rachel to bring up the rear.

Okay, lesson learned: I still liked dogs better than kids. And just because I'd managed to make a friend out of one mixed-up girl with dark hair and a bad attitude did not mean I'd cornered the market on child psychology.

Moving on.

~

As the sun rose, our little line of hikers spread out, the chatter grew more sporadic, and the thirty five-plus pound packs the kids carried began to take their toll. I was reminded that three months of sleeping late, lounging around the house, and eating fast food had left me in considerably less than tip-top shape. After the first hour, I took Cisco's backpack off and carried it myself for the next hour, because he hadn't had any more time to condition himself to this kind of exercise than I had. The temperature hit forty (I know because I surreptitiously checked the app on my phone) and I tied my jacket around my waist, advising the kids to do the same before they started to sweat. I figured that much was within my purview as a wilderness survival expert.

I munched on trail mix, sipped water from the pouch on my backpack, and fed Cisco some high-protein treats. After we had been hiking for three hours, we came to the first challenge: a steep-banked creek that was too wide to jump and too deep to wade across. I assumed the kids were supposed to figure out how to build a bridge to the other side using ropes and fallen logs, but I knew that no matter what kind of bridge they came up with, Cisco would not cross it. So while the others arrived one by one, wearily divested themselves of their packs, and began to discuss the best way to cross, Cisco and I went downstream in search of the shallows.

It's true I had never been on this trail before, but I was familiar enough with the terrain to know that if I walked far enough the banks would eventually flatten out; that was the nature of mountain streams. I was in luck. After ten or fifteen minutes of hiking I could easily climb down the bank and jump across the stream in two quick steps that didn't even splash the bottom of my jeans and barely stained my waterproof boots. Cisco happily padded across without even getting his white feathers wet. We climbed up the opposite bank and hiked back up stream.

Along the way, I took out my phone and texted Melanie.

Don't ever get a tattoo.

She texted back: *Kewl! I want a paw print.*

Terrific. I was sure Miles would be thrilled when Melanie started pestering him to let her get a paw print tattoo, and there would be no use pretending I'd had nothing to do with it. On the other hand, the good news was that Miles had been right: even out here in the middle of nowhere, the phone worked perfectly.

We could hear the kids' voices on the other side long before we saw them, and they did not sound happy. One of the girls said, "Why can't we just camp here?"

And another one—it sounded like Lourdes—spoke over her: "If you think I'm going to crawl over that rickety-looking thing, you're stupider than you look, boy."

One of the boys snapped back, "If you'd both just shut up and give us a hand—"

It was then that Cisco, excited to see his friends on the other side, pushed through the underbrush to the edge of the bank and barked a happy greeting.

Jess and Pete were trying to roll a log from a fallen tree—which, by the way, looked about six inches too short to span the creek—to the bank. Everyone else was sitting on the ground, munching protein bars. When they saw Cisco on the other side of the creek, the astonishment on their faces made me grin.

"Hey," I said. "If one of y'all will toss me a rope I'll tie it off on this side and we can haul your backpacks over. It'll be easier than trying to walk that tree with them on."

One of the girls—Angel, I thought it was—swallowed the half-chewed bite of her protein bar and demanded indignantly, "How did you do that?"

And Pete, straightening up from his efforts with the log, echoed, "Yeah, how did you get over there?"

"There's a crossing about a quarter mile downstream," I explained companionably. "My dog doesn't do bridges."

"Yeah, well, I don't do bridges either," said Lourdes, scowling.

Jess dropped his end of the log. "The hell with this," he said. Hoisting his backpack, he raised his arm in a kind of lazy salute and declared, "Troops onward!"

He started trudging downstream, and the others scrambled to get their possessions together to follow him. It wasn't until I saw the quiet fury churning in the eyes of Paul Evans that I realized I had screwed up. Royally.

Of course there was no going back from there. The kids found the shallow crossing as easily as I had and were soon once again marching along the trail, their spirits somewhat higher for having cheated destiny and greatly reassured by the promise that the camp site was less than an hour's walk away. It was forty-two degrees with four hours of sunlight left. Not bad for the first day.

Paul caught up with me when we had all been on the trail again for less than five minutes. "The point, Miss Stockton," he said lowly, "was for our students to use the skills they have acquired over the past six weeks in the program to work together and build a bridge. Your interference was counterproductive."

I replied innocently, "I'm sorry. I thought the point was to cross the stream."

Rick, my boss at the forest service, used to say I was lucky we had gone to high school together, because I was such a smart-ass no one else would ever hire me. Maybe he was right. Because I do tend to say what I think about any given situation, and I don't have a lot of patience for idiots.

"I thought we made it clear you were not to interfere with our therapy program," he said sternly.

"And I thought I was hired as a wilderness expert," I replied. "Do you want me to do my job or not?"

He gave me one of those gut-freezing looks that reminded me of the times I had been called into the principal's office as a kid. For the first time, I felt sorry for the young people in his charge.

But he said nothing. He let me out-distance him with my stride, and I could feel his eyes boring into my back, as though he was trying without success to think of a rejoinder. Later, it occurred to me that that was probably the first time anyone had successfully talked back to him.

I felt a little smug for that. I'm not proud to admit it, but I did.

CHAPTER EIGHT

We reached the first day's campsite while the sun was still high and hazy-bright in the western sky. Lourdes had, of course, fallen far behind once again, but no one seemed to miss her. They got busy setting up camp just as though they knew what they were doing, and I left them to it.

Paul had made it clear the staff was not to help with any of the physical aspects of setting up camp, so I unleashed my two-step pop-up tent, staked it down securely into the frozen ground, unrolled my sleeping bag over the foam pad, set up my camp stove, and poured food and water into Cisco's collapsible bowls. While he lapped up the contents of both bowls, I sat cross-legged on the sleeping bag and prepared a gourmet MRE of not-half-bad chili, followed by a tube of orange-pineapple sherbet for dessert. Always pay extra for the good stuff.

I crawled out of the tent, surprised at the drop in temperature that had occurred in the short time I'd been inside. The sun had started to sink behind a mountain peak and the wind had picked up with a bitter bite. The kids were struggling to assemble their own tents, swearing and whining, but I ignored them as instructed. I flipped up the hood of my jacket and tightened the drawstrings, pulling on my gloves while I walked Cisco into the wood line. Once away from the camp, I attached a twenty-foot line to Cisco's collar, and allowed him to claim his own doggie latrine. While he was so occupied, I took my phone from my pocket and checked my messages. There was one from Maude, reporting that all was well, one from Melanie wanting to know how, exactly, to teach a dog to speak who wasn't old enough to bark—as though I hadn't tried to warn her about that exact problem—and one from Miles, leaving his hotel contact information. I called Melanie back.

She answered chirpily.

"May I speak with Pepper?" I asked politely.

She giggled and there was a lot of clunking and static, but in a moment the goofy face of a golden retriever puppy appeared on the screen. You've got to respect a kid who always knows where her puppy is.

In the background I could hear Melanie prompting, "Speak, Pepper, speak!"

Pepper sniffed the camera and turned around to chew her tail.

"Pepper," I said seriously, "I want you to be patient with your new mom, who loves you very much. Sometimes she forgets you are a dog. We all know that you'll show her how smart you are when you learn to bark on command in three or four months, but in the meantime maybe you could save us all some time by teaching *her* to walk by your side without tightening the leash in public. That would be great. Now could I speak with Melanie again?"

When Melanie's face came back on the screen it was a mixture of amusement and, I was happy to see, a little bit of chagrin. "Pepper says she'll think about it," she said.

"Good for her."

"My dad says you're pretty smart," she added.

I liked that. "Yeah, well, what do you think?"

"I think you're kind of a nut."

I laughed. "Listen, Melanie, I'm out here in the middle of nowhere so I might not be able to call you every day. But if you need anything you can call me because I'm checking my messages all the time, okay?"

"Okay. Dad says we're coming back to the mountains next month."

"Cool. Are you having fun with Grandma?"

"You bet. She lets me watch Animal Planet until bed time. Did you know there are 300 species of venomous snakes in the world?"

"Did not know that," I admitted. And, if I were to be completely honest, it wasn't the kind of thing I really wanted floating around in my head while hiking the wilderness, even if it was the dead of winter. "I've got to get back to work. Tell Pepper bye for me, okay?"

"Okay," she responded happily. "I'll text you."

I chuckled. "Okay. Bye, Melanie."

As I was about to put the phone away, it buzzed in my hand. When I hit the answer button, Miles's face appeared on the screen, looking well-rested and well-groomed against a late evening backdrop of cerulean ocean and gold and azure sky. He said, "What's this I hear about you and Melanie getting matching paw print tattoos?'

I tightened my hood and turned my back against a sudden gust of icy wind. "Are you on your hotel balcony?"

He lifted a glass of something frothy and tropical looking to me. "Why, sugar, you look cold."

"Do you know how much I hate you right now?"

He chuckled. "I guess I shouldn't ask how it's going, then."

I noticed that the quality of the video wasn't quite what it had been the last time we'd talked, but I didn't know whether that was due to my altitude or the international transmission. I said, "Promise me you'll never send Melanie to boot camp."

There was a stutter of broken pixels, and all I caught was something about a tattoo. Then the video caught up with the audio and he added, "Sorry to hear it's not as much fun as you thought it would be. I can't imagine why."

"I almost got fired twice today. Somebody put a bottle of bourbon in Cisco's backpack. One of the juvies called me a bitch and threatened to cut me. My boss's wife hates me. My boss hates me. Every muscle in my body aches. Even my fingernails are cold."

He took a sip of his drink. "I had lobster for

dinner."

"I'm going to hang up."

"Did I ever tell you about my condo in St. Bart's? It's got a hot tub *and* a sauna."

"Right now I'd settle for a hot bath."

"No offense, hon, but you do look a little like something from *The Blair Witch Project*."

I stuck out my tongue at him and he said, "Now I'm really scared."

"You should be." I shivered against another blast of wind. Then I lowered my voice a little, frowning with uncertainty, and I added, "Miles, I'm no child psychiatrist, and I never even *heard* of wilderness outreach therapy until the day before yesterday, but I'm not all that wild about the way this program is run. I mean, if I treated my clients' dogs this way, I'd be out of business in a month."

The silence that followed might have been a product of the international connection, but there was no mistaking the somberness of his expression. "Listen," he said, "I know you hate it when I interfere."

"Yes," I agreed, "I do." After a little over three month's acquaintance, the one thing I knew for sure was that Miles and I got along best when we stayed out of each other's business. On the other hand, he was one of the smartest men I knew, so I added, only a little reluctantly, "What have you got?"

"I had a few minutes between meetings so I did a little research on this outfit. I couldn't figure out why I'd never heard of them. It turns out they've only been in business eight months."

"But…" I was exhausted and my brain was numb with cold, but I was certain that wasn't right. "Paul told me they had been here three years."

"And that property with the lodge that looks so great on the website? It's rented."

"Rented? Are you sure?"

"Honey, I'm in the real estate business. I'm sure. I talked to the owner. It's a long term lease, with cash up front, but it's rented."

I wasn't certain what was more confusing: the lies Paul Evans had told or the trouble Miles had gone to on my behalf. "You talked to the owner?"

"There's something else." His tone was grim. "Last fall the New Day Wilderness Program made the news when one of their counselors went missing."

I rubbed my forehead, which was beginning to ache. "I know. It was in Bullard, which was why I wasn't called in on the search. But they found him in a couple of days."

"They found him, all right," Miles said. "Dead."

I stared at the image on the screen. I thought, *Damn it.* And again, with more vehemence, *Damn it.* If my esteemed ex-husband and the acting sheriff of Hanover County had been on duty where he belonged instead of chasing skirt in Florida, he would have taken my call and I would have known that little detail before I climbed halfway up a mountain in thirty degree temperatures with a couple of people who may or may not be who they claimed to be. It wasn't as though I hadn't tried to do my research.

"Damn it," I said out loud, through gritted teeth.

"Apparently he left the expedition in the middle, but never made it back to town. The death was ruled accidental, but I thought you'd want to know. I'll send you the article."

I passed a hand over my face, trying to regain my composure. "Yeah, thanks. That'd be great. When are you coming back?"

"A couple of days. I'll check with you when I get back to the States."

"I have to keep my phone off during the day. We're supposed to be incommunicado."

"I'm starting to think you should have gotten paid up front."

Cisco wound his way through the brush back to me and I reached down to rub his neck. "Me, too."

"By the way, you'll want to keep your eye on the weather. There's a storm front headed your way."

"Not possible. I checked the forecast before I left."

"It'll probably play out before it reaches you, but Houston is already iced in."

I groaned. "Terrific. And you know this from Portugal?"

"That's why they call it the World Wide Web." A pause. "You okay?"

I sighed. "Yeah. I'm good. And listen… thanks. You know, for interfering."

He winked at me. "Any time. Bundle up, sweetie."

"Don't worry," I told him. "I've got my best guy to snuggle with." I turned the phone to Cisco's face, who swiped the screen with his tongue. I heard Miles laughing just before he disconnected.

I turned to go back to camp saw Rachel standing with her feet planted and her hands in her pockets about ten feet away. Her expression was pinched and frozen looking, her eyes radiated disapproval, and I felt like a kid who had been caught in the back seat of her boyfriend's car. I didn't know how much, if anything she had heard, nor did I particularly care. Needless to say, I was not in a very receptive mood as I approached her.

"Miss Stockton," she said, "There is a reason we don't allow cell phones on these expeditions."

Cisco, his tail waving enthusiastically, hurried forward to greet her, but I grabbed his collar. I said, "I'd love to know what it is. I've always thought of a cell phone as a necessary piece of emergency equipment for any wilderness expedition."

A faint expression of wariness crossed her face as she glanced at Cisco, but once she was certain I had him under control, she looked back at me. "Many of our students are from families of influence and wealth—politicians, celebrities, even royalty. We don't have the kind of security system that can keep them safe in a place like this and a single photo posted to Twitter could put them at risk for kidnapping or worse."

I'll admit, I hadn't thought of that. Before I could assure her that she needn't worry about anything of the sort from me, she went on, "Aside from that—and perhaps of more immediate concern—these children are here because they have in one way or another come up against the law. The minute they find out you have a cell phone is the minute you can kiss it good-bye, because there isn't a kid here who wouldn't relieve you of it the first chance he got and use it to call his dealer, his brother, his best friend or even his dad to come and get him. All else aside, you can see how that might present more of a danger up here than it would in the nice safe compound below."

I understood perfectly. A teenager who believed rescue was on the way—or who at least had access to the outside world—might be far more inclined to take off on his own than someone who was isolated and dependent on others for his survival. I was ready to apologize and promise to keep my phone turned off and securely zipped in the innermost pocket of my pack when she held out her gloved hand, palm up, like a teacher confiscating contraband from a wayward student.

I stared at her hand. I stared at her frosty gray eyes. And then I couldn't help it; I laughed out loud, mostly from sheer surprise, but also because of the absurdity of it. She couldn't have been much older than I was, she was paying me to be here, and she was treating me like one of her troubled teenagers. I said, "I don't think so," and started to move past her.

She closed her fingers around my arm. "I'm afraid I must insist."

My amusement turned to disbelief, and then to cool indignation. I pulled my arm away, slowly but deliberately. I said, "I appreciate your concern, but I'll take care of it myself. Cisco, with me."

I moved past her toward the camp, and I could feel her eyes boring into me with every step. She was clearly a woman who was not accustomed to being refused, and I supposed that was only natural in her line of work. At least that was what I told myself. Because the other possibility was far more unpalatable, if a great deal more likely: Rachel Evans was, quite simply, a bully.

CHAPTER NINE

The sun was a fuzzy white remnant filtered through skeletal tree limbs when I reached the camp. The shadows on the ground were long and cold. Most of the tents were erected, though Pete was still pounding down the stakes on his. Tiffanie and Jess had scraped out a shallow fire pit and Jess dropped an armload of sticks into it. They were arguing about something as I approached, which hardly surprised me. I glanced at the sticks Jess had tossed in the pit and suggested, "Try not to get wood that's been lying on the ground. It soaks up water from the leaves and it won't burn. Look for dead branches caught in bushes or on low limbs of trees."

Jess slanted me a dark glance and Tiffanie retorted, "See, dumbass? You couldn't make a fire even *with* matches!"

Angel crawled out of her tent. "I looked all

through my pack. I couldn't find any."

Jess shouted, "Hey, Pete! You got any matches?" He strode toward Pete's tent.

I said to the girls, "There's a deadfall a couple of dozen yards into the woods to the west. You'll find plenty of dry wood there." I glanced around. "Where's Lourdes?"

"Still back there, I guess." Tiffanie gestured impatiently back down the trail. "She'll be lucky if she gets here by morning. Come on, Angel. Let's go get the wood Jess should have gotten in the first place." She raised her voice on the last to make certain Jess overheard, and Jess turned to make an obscene gesture with his fist.

"Wait a minute," I said as the girls started toward the woods. "Do you mean Lourdes isn't back yet? Seriously?"

"So what's so surprising about that?" Angel said, trudging on.

I marched Cisco over to Paul, who was checking the security of the girls' tent stakes.

"Lourdes isn't back yet," I said.

He glanced up at me. "That's right."

"But all the counselors are here. You said we were supposed to keep the kids in sight."

"Lourdes chose her own pace. She also chose

the consequences."

I stared at him. "It's getting dark. She's alone on a trail that's hard enough to see in the daylight and you just *left* her?"

"She has a flashlight and an emergency whistle."

"Are you freaking kidding me?" It had been a long day. My voice rose in pitch. "Do you have any idea how many times I've gone into the mountains looking for people who *started out* with flashlights and emergency whistles?"

Cisco, sensing my tension, or perhaps a little on edge himself, sat at my side and barked. The boys nudged each other and grinned in the way kids do when they catch adults behaving inappropriately. I probably should have been embarrassed, or at least a little apologetic for yelling at my boss. But I knew exactly who was going to go back down the trail with a flashlight looking for Lourdes if she didn't show up within the next hour, and I wasn't the least bit inclined to apologize to Paul Evans.

Paul said calmly, "One of the things we try to teach our students while they're with us is the importance of making correct choices. I would appreciate it if you would not interfere with that lesson. I suspect she'll be back before the boys get the campfire lit."

Jess said, "Umm, about that... anybody got a match?"

I ignored him, my gaze fastened hard on Paul. It was clearly past time we cleared up a few things. "Could I speak with you privately?"

His eyes flickered over my shoulder and then back to me. I knew without turning around that Rachel had come up behind me. She said, "Group session starts in twenty minutes, gentlemen. If you don't get the fire started pretty soon, you won't have time to eat."

Pete said impatiently, "Look, nobody can find any matches, so either you guys forgot to pack them or—"

"I assure you, Mr. Randall, we packed plenty of matches."

"Oh, for Heaven's sake." I turned sharply to him, digging into my pocket for matches. Then I stopped. "Do you mean none of you kids packed your own backpacks?"

"Of course not." Jess's tone was snide, and he hunched his shoulders and shivered in the wind. "We might try to sneak in some contraband chocolate."

Rachel saw my hand on the matches and said,

"It's important to let the students solve their own problems, Miss Stockton."

"Yeah, well, let me know when somebody figures out how to solve this one." Jess turned and started to stomp back to his tent.

I said, "Wait a minute."

Jess looked at me impatiently. Rachel said in a warning tone, "Miss Stockton…"

I ignored her. "You're supposed to be in charge," I said to Jess. "You can go back to your tent and let everyone go cold and hungry tonight. Or you can use your brain and figure this out."

"What?" he demanded irritably. "You going to teach us how to rub two sticks together or something?"

"You checked all the backpacks for matches, right?"

"I told you that."

"*All* of them?"

He made a hissing sound of dismissal through his teeth and started to turn away again. Then understanding dawned. He looked at Pete. "They put all the matches in Lard-Ass's pack." He turned to Paul and demanded, "Didn't you? You knew she'd be the last one here and you just wanted to see us suffer."

"I didn't know that," Paul replied mildly. "I had no possible way of knowing that. If you had helped her keep up this afternoon, she would have arrived at the same time as everyone else, and you'd have a fire by now."

"Son of a—" The way he cut himself off made me think he had already learned that the penalty for swearing was even worse than going to bed without supper.

Pete said miserably, "We might as well give up on getting anything hot to eat, then. By the time she gets here we'll all be asleep—or frozen. I'm too tired to eat anyway."

Jess said angrily, "I'm sick of you people and your stupid games."

I held his gaze and said softly, "Wouldn't you like to win one for a change?"

Jess glared at me, then at Paul. Without another word, he swung away from us both and started back down the trail.

"Where are you going?" Pete demanded.

"Where do you think?" he tossed back. "To find Lourdes!"

~

Cisco and I went with him, of course, and, after

a moment's discussion with Rachel, Paul caught up with us. What bothered me was the suspicion that, if I had not decided to follow Jess, Paul would have let him go alone.

No wonder they needed a survival expert on this expedition.

The shadows grew deeper and the wind grew colder the farther down the trail we went. Lourdes was only a fifteen minute walk down the trail, but for someone who was cold, tired and hungry, it was fifteen minutes too long. She was little more than a shadow among shadows, sitting beside her discarded pack with her head resting on her up-drawn knees. Cisco and I were in the lead, with Jess walking in silent anger beside me, and Paul only a few feet behind. When he saw her, Jess pushed ahead of me. Paul caught my arm before I could go with him.

I pulled my arm away. "Don't worry," I said, watching Jess, "I won't interfere with your precious treatment program."

"We've been doing this a long time. We know what works."

I turned to look at him. "You've been doing this," I replied distinctly, "precisely eight months. Why did you tell me you'd been in Hanover

County three years?"

In the dim and fading light, his expression was difficult to read. But his tone did not change as he assured me easily, "I told you we had been in business for three years. We've been at our present location since May of last year."

I was almost certain he had not said that at all. But I was tired and cold and most of my attention was on Jess and Lourdes, and there was just enough doubt to prevent me from arguing about it. Besides, this was not the time or the place.

Lourdes looked up as Jess approached and scrubbed at her face with both hands. Jess strode up to her, grabbed her pack from the ground, and began searching the pockets.

"What are you doing?" she demanded. But her voice lacked both the force and the petulance it had held earlier in the day. In fact, it sounded wet and weak and all but defeated.

Jess dropped her pack and turned triumphantly with a plastic baggie of matches in his hand. "Got it!" he declared. He started to walk away.

There was a note of panic in Lourdes' voice as she said, "Where are you going?" She pushed herself to her feet. "Are you leaving?"

Jess kept walking.

I bent down and unclipped Cisco's leash, whispering a command into his ear.

Cisco trotted down the trail past Jess, and Jess turned to watch as the golden retriever walked right up to Lourdes and took her sleeve in his mouth. Gently he began to tug, urging her forward.

It was a trick we performed to entertain school children when we did programs for libraries and classrooms on pet care and education. It always made the kids laugh. But Lourdes wasn't laughing. After an astonished moment she took one step forward, and then another. I could hear a quavering in her voice as she said, "Good dog." She awkwardly reached down to pet Cisco's neck. "Good dog."

Jess scowled at me and then at the matches in his hand. I returned a calm and steady gaze because I knew that, somewhere deep inside, he wasn't as bad as he pretended to be. He pushed past me angrily, pretending not to notice. Cisco and I walked silently back to camp with Lourdes, Paul bringing up the rear. I couldn't help noticing that Jess never got too far ahead, and he would glance back every few minutes just to make sure we were still there.

The kids built an impressive bonfire that warmed the ground for yards around and it cast a happy glow into the woods beyond as the sun began to set. It was, unfortunately, too large and too hot for cooking, but they had worked so hard and so enthusiastically making trip after trip into the deadfall to bring back armloads of fuel that, when Rachel pointed out their folly, I couldn't stand to see their expressions fall once again.

"Why don't you just build a separate cooking fire?" I suggested. "You've got plenty of wood, and you don't have to dig another pit. Just line it with some of those flat rocks, and be sure to bury the embers when you're done."

Lourdes and Pete, whose names had come up first in meal prep rotation, looked pleased with that solution, and everyone else was relieved that their meal would not be delayed until the big fire died down enough to cook on.

But Rachel's eyes flared with impatience and her tone was tight as she said, "Consequences, Miss Stockton."

I was really getting a little tired of that. It occurred to me that if one of the goals of this program was to build confidence, it probably wouldn't hurt to let the kids succeed at something once in a while. So I replied simply, "Dinner, Mrs. Evans."

She turned away without replying, but if looks could really speak, her words would have all had four letters.

~

The kids ate some kind of lukewarm, pre-packaged goulash that even Cisco sniffed and ignored and gathered around the bonfire as the sun died for an evaluation of the day's performance. I unfolded a space blanket for Cisco and sat beside him, brushing the burrs out of his coat while he cuddled with his stuffed rabbit. One by one, the kids reviewed the day: the best part, the worst part, the things they could have done better. For Jess, the best part of the day was that it was over, the worst part was dinner, and as for what he could have done better—not a damn thing. That, of course, set the tone, and no one took the exercise seriously after that. It seemed to me that Rachel would have known better than to let Jess start.

I had finished brushing Cisco and was into a gentle game of tug with his rabbit when Paul said,

"Miss Stockton, would you like to comment on what we can all learn from our first day on the trail?"

Oh, there was plenty I could have said, but I decided it would probably be best to confine my comments to my own area of expertise. So I released Cisco's toy to him and said, "Okay, sure. There are a lot of things you should have learned today." I looked around the fire-lit faces of the weary, miserable and disinterested teenagers and said, "The first one is that there is always more than one way around an obstacle on the trail. Think about the animals, the deer and raccoon and bears. They don't build bridges across streams. They look for the path of least resistance. You should too."

The kids seemed to like that—probably because they knew I had been reprimanded for suggesting that they go downstream to cross, instead of building a bridge over the stream. They thought they had gotten away with something, but I wasn't the one who had made them feel that way; Paul had. They paid a bit more attention now.

"Secondly…" I fixed a meaningful look on Jess and Pete. "Always pack your own backpack. You boys had everything you own scattered on the ground this morning, you had every opportunity to check the contents of your pack, and neither one of you noticed you didn't have any matches. What happened was your own fault." Angel suppressed a giggle and tried to be subtle about elbowing Tiffanie, but both of the boys noticed and scowled.

Their good mood was gone, but I wasn't finished. "As for leaving a team member behind…" Now my gaze went to each and every one of them, including Rachel and Paul, who certainly got no latitude from me on this point. "That's not only mean, but dangerous and stupid. If even one of you so much as sprains an ankle, all of you could freeze to death. Do you get that?" Well, okay, so I exaggerated a little—we weren't on Mt. Everest, after all—but that got their attention. The girls looked uneasily toward Lourdes, who stared fixedly at the fire, and the boys hunched their shoulders and shifted their gazes, the way boys do when they're ashamed and defensive. "And finally," I concluded, feeling I'd earned my wages for the day, "just so you know—don't ever, and I mean *ever*…" This time I looked right at Paul. "Have one person carry all of an essential survival supply. What if Lourdes had slipped in the stream this afternoon and gotten the matches wet? What if she had lost her backpack somehow? Just take a minute and think about what you'd all be doing now."

Their faces, in the orange firelight, look sober—all except Paul's, which looked quietly furious. Well, I couldn't blame him. He'd look like a fool if he disagreed with me, but if he didn't disagree, he would look like a fool for hiring me. Still, he had been wrong. And I wasn't quite as anxious to impress either him or his wife as I had been before I'd started this job.

I said, "Before you turn in tonight, I suggest each one of you check your gear. Make sure you have everything in your backpack you'll need to survive in case you get separated from the group. That includes matches. And oh, by the way, you'd better hope you *don't* get separated from the group."

I saw Paul open his mouth to speak, and—possibly because I can be a little petty, possibly because I really did still have the floor—I said, "One more thing. Drink plenty of water. Keep a bottle in your sleeping bag tonight, but don't refill your pouches until the morning. Otherwise, your water will freeze."

I tried to watch Paul's face, but I was distracted by a groan from Tiffanie and a giggle from Angel.

"The world's smallest bladder," Angel said, pointing to Tiffanie.

"And I'm not getting up to go in the middle of the night," Tiffanie said. "There are animals and stuff in the woods, and besides, it's cold."

"Gonna get colder if you pee your sleeping bag," Pete jeered, and Tiffanie found a small pebble to toss across the fire at him. He ducked, of course.

I said, "Get up. Go. There are no animals in the woods this time of year that are interested in you. Just take your flashlight."

The kids started to stir in preparation for rising, and Paul said, "One more thing before you go. You need to elect a leader for tomorrow's hike."

I'm sure that this was an important part of the therapy program, and most likely teachable moments occurred every night over the campfire while the team members debated the merits of their leader's performance that day. In the summertime, I'm sure that was the case. But it was full dark at six o'clock, the fire was dying down and the wind was blowing in from the northern mountain peaks and all the kids wanted to do was get in their sleeping bags. The silence that followed resonated.

At last Lourdes said sourly, "If you ask me, the only one of you worth keeping is that dog."

Cisco looked up alertly from his dedicated grooming of the rabbit, which made a few of them smile. Somebody must have clucked his tongue, because Cisco got up then, his stuffed rabbit in his mouth and his tail swishing proudly, and started going around the circle from person to person, as though campaigning for votes. I let his leash drop and chuckled with the others as tensions eased. This is why they call them therapy dogs.

"All right, enough," Rachel said sharply. "You know the rules. No one goes to bed before you decide on tomorrow's hike leader."

And the fun was over. I extended my hand to Cisco and whistled softly. He came back to the space blanket and flopped down, grinning up at me.

Tiffanie said impatiently, "Whatever. Jess didn't kill anybody today, let him do it. Who cares?"

"Yeah, who cares?' said someone else, and another added, "Whatever."

"The people have spoken," Jess said, yawning broadly as he stood. "Whatever."

I could see that Rachel wanted to argue, or at least issue another command, but she was the one who had insisted they vote. And, as Jess said, the people had spoken.

It took barely half an hour for the kids to clean up the remnants of dinner and disperse. By seven o'clock, we were all in our tents, and by seven thirty, voices had quieted and lanterns had been extinguished. I ran the camp stove for a few minutes, just to take the bite out of the air, then dived in my sleeping bag and settled Cisco on the space blanket right next to me. I was lucky. Between the two of us, we would generate enough heat to keep the tent almost cozy all night. The others, even with their expensive camping gear, could very likely look forward to a miserable expanse of hours before morning.

I was so tired that I could barely keep my eyes open, but I made myself dig my phone out of my backpack and, pulling the edges of the sleeping bag up around my ears, I scrolled down until I found the e-mailed article Miles had sent. It was from the Bullard *Daily News*, which was in fact a weekly newspaper, and it was brief and to the point:

MISSING CAMPER FOUND DEAD
Oct. 15

The body of 26-year-old Brian Maddox of Pendleton, Ohio, was found Thursday at the bottom of a ravine in the Attahachee Wilderness Area, the apparent victim of an accidental fall.

Maddox was reported missing last week after he failed to return from a hiking expedition with the New Day Wilderness Program for troubled youth, where he was employed as a counselor. According to witnesses, Maddox left the expedition shortly after it began without notice after an apparent dispute over wages. Maddox had been employed with New Day Wilderness Program, which is headquartered in Hansonville, North Carolina, for three months.

His body will be returned to Pendleton, Ohio, for burial.

My brain reacted slowly. I thought, *Why do I know that name?* And then I thought, *Pendleton, Ohio.* I almost missed the photo at the bottom of the article. The pleasant face of the blond haired young man who came into view made me frown because I knew it was familiar. In fact, something about the entire photo, which, with its blurry details and grainy resolution, was clearly a detail enlarged from another picture, was very familiar to me. And as I scrolled down, I knew why.

I had seen it in the New Day year book.

The young man's hand was resting on the head of a black Lab with a white star on his chest. I might be a little slow with human faces, but I recognized the dog immediately. The dog's name was Max, and he was right now snoozing away in radiantly-heated comfort at my newly renovated kennel.

CHAPTER TEN

After that, sleep did not come easily. I lay awake watching the wind fretfully toss the skeletal shadows of tree limbs across the face of my tent and listening to the snap and crackle of the canvas, trying to remember where I had heard the name of Brian Maddox before. By the time I figured it out, it was too late to call Maude and ask her to confirm my speculation by looking up the phone records, so my mind turned to worrying about another question: how had Heather ended up with Max, the dog of the boy who had died on a hike very similar to this one six months ago, and why had she lied about Max's real identity?

I fell into an exhausted, if uneasy, sleep to the sound of Cisco's peaceful snoring.

I awoke with a start to the sound of a low and ominous growling. Believe me, this is one thing you do not want to hear in the dark in the middle of the woods with nothing standing between you and your Maker except a few millimeters of canvas and a loyal golden retriever. Instinctively, I put my hand out to rest on Cisco's shoulder. Usually, my touch will calm him, but I could feel the tension in his muscles and, as my eyes adjusted to the dark, I could see him staring alertly toward the front of the tent. And then I heard another sound. It took me a moment to identify it as the sound of my tent door being unzipped from the outside.

A lot of things happened very quickly after that. Cisco stood up and barked sharply. I said (actually I intended to shout, but it came out as a hoarse croak), "Who's there?" There was some scrambling outside and Cisco rushed to the tent flap—less than one stride for him—and nosed the opening while I disentangled myself from my sleeping bag and pushed my feet into my boots. And then I heard a scream.

I grabbed my flashlight and switched it on. The minute I unzipped the flap, Cisco burst through. I was half a step behind him.

I stumbled out into a navy blue night with my flashlight beam all but blinding me. I heard voices, one of them crying, "I'm bleeding! I'm hurt!" I caught a glimpse of Cisco's white furry tail spinning into the night. I plunged forward after him.

I saw Heather coming from the right and Rachel coming from the left. I heard the sound of tents unzipping as I passed and sleepy unhappy voices demanded, "What the…" Cisco bounded straight to the figure on the ground, about fifteen feet from my tent. Tiffanie had a hand pressed to her cheek and I could see the dark smear of blood between her fingertips.

Heather was there before me, kneeling before Tiffanie, speaking softly to her. Cisco was already there, eagerly investigating the scene and, to be frank, mostly getting in the way. I caught his collar.

"What happened?" I demanded. "What were you doing, trying to break into my tent?"

"Somebody pushed me!" Tiffanie was crying now, more scared than hurt, I suspected, as Heather helped her to a sitting position. And then she glared at me. "What are you talking about? I was nowhere near your tent!" She pulled her hand away from her face, saw the blood in the reflection of my flashlight beam and squealed again. "I'm bleeding! Someone pushed me!"

Rachel arrived then and knelt beside Tiffanie, impatiently pushing Heather away. "What happened?"

"I was going… I went to use the latrine and I was coming back. Someone pushed me and I fell… is it bad? Will there be a scar? I'm bleeding!"

I swept the ground with my flashlight beam for Tiffanie's flashlight and found it, a half dozen steps away, where it had come to rest against a small rock. I tried the switch and got nothing. It was broken. I brought it back to Tiffanie.

Clearly, she was not the person who had tried to break into my tent. She couldn't have gotten this far away in the few seconds that had passed, and from the direction in which her flashlight had rolled, I could tell she had been coming toward camp, as she claimed, and not away from it.

Paul had arrived by then and the others were slowly crawling out of their tents. There was a lot of noise. Cisco lunged forward to put his nose in Tiffanie's face. Tiffanie grabbed hold of his fur for a moment, and then turned toward Rachel's ministrations.

I said, "Someone tried to unzip my tent a minute ago. That's what woke Cisco up. Tiffanie, did you see anyone?"

Rachel cast me an incredulous look. Paul's look was more like that of someone who was at the end of his rope. Tiffanie whined, "I'm hurt. I want to go home."

"You're not hurt," Rachel said calmly, helping her to her feet. "You're barely scratched. You just tripped. Come back to my tent and we'll put some ointment on it. You're fine."

Paul turned to the others, who had begun to gather like reluctant ravens on a wire in their long-johns and boots, shivering in the cold. "It's okay, everybody. She's fine. Reveille at sunrise. Who has kitchen duty?"

The others turned away, grumbling, to go back to their tents, and even I was feeling the bite of the sub-freezing night through the silk long johns and cable-knit sweater I'd worn to bed. Tiffanie was wearing her coat, which made sense, since she had had time to put one on before she left her tent. Oddly enough, so was Rachel.

And, I noticed as she quickly hurried away, so was Heather.

~

There are a lot of things that can impair your judgment, put you in danger, and generally take all the fun out of a winter hiking expedition. The first and most obvious is probably alcohol consumption. Second would have to be dehydration and/or lack of adequate nutrition—which, believe it or not, can be a huge problem in the kinds of extreme conditions you're likely to encounter on a winter hike. Third, and probably the most common, is sleep deprivation.

By the time all the commotion settled, I figure I got probably four hours of sleep that night. And that was *with* a warm blooded, furry companion who heated up the tent and made falling asleep again a lot easier than it would have otherwise been. Nonetheless, I was awake again at the barest hint of dawn. I pulled on jeans, boots, and jacket, and with blurry eyes and cold-numb fingers, made my way to the human latrine, and then to the doggie one, in the green-gray light of a dying night.

When I returned to the campsite, there were a few shadows stirring about, as was the smell of smoky green wood, the clank of collapsible metal cooking pots. The campsite itself was small and precise, with the tents close together and the fire pit in the center; all around we were surrounded by woods and brush. Behind my tent, so that I would only notice it as I approached from the opposite direction, was a stand of scrub pine. And on a low branch of one of those pines was something odd.

Cisco, with his keen twilight vision and natural curiosity, was the first to notice, and he pulled ahead on his leash toward a pile of white fluff at the base of a tree next to the tent. I was more interested in the object that was hanging from the branch and which, as I came closer, looked so much like a dead animal that my throat actually tightened with alarm and my heart skipped a beat. And then I saw it.

Cisco's stuffed rabbit was hanging crookedly by its neck from a shoelace tied to a pine branch. It had been eviscerated, and the stuffing on the ground was the white fluff that Cisco was so eagerly investigating. Attached to the corpse of the rabbit with a straight pin was a note scrawled on the back of a protein bar wrapper. It read:

And your little dog too

You know that thing I said about dog trainers being able to stay calm in a crisis? It doesn't apply when my dog is threatened. My first instinct was to grab the effigy and march back to the cooking fire, roaring at everyone in sight and demanding a confession. If I could have found the sick SOB who was responsible, I honestly don't know what I would have done, but threats and warnings would not have been all that were on the agenda. This was my dog. This was Cisco. This was not acceptable.

I was in such a white rage that I was ready to confront the entire group at the top of my lungs in my next breath, but then I heard Jess's voice by my shoulder. "Whoa, pooch. Who'd you piss off?"

I whirled on him, but all I saw in his face was a kind of horrified disbelief. Lourdes came up beside him, looked over the situation, and her face slowly darkened with fury. "You think this is funny?" she said lowly.

Jess lifted both hands in self-defense, "Hey, not me."

She grabbed the stuffed rabbit from the tree and jerked it loose, whirling back toward the sleepy forms that were emerging from the tents. "Which one of you stupid jackasses thinks this is funny?" she yelled. "He's just a dog! He didn't do nothing to any of you!"

And even though she was saying exactly what I wanted to say, I reached out quickly to place a calming hand on her arm. "Lourdes, it's just a joke. I'm sure—"

She jerked her arm away, not even looking at me. "You're all a bunch of pathetic losers, all of you! He's just a dog!"

She tossed the toy on the ground and stomped away.

By this time it was light enough for everyone to see what she was talking about, and for me to carefully watch their reactions. As I've said, I don't know much about teenagers, aside from the fact that I was once one. But I do know the one thing they all have in common is an absolute inability to keep a secret, particularly when it comes to a practical joke. But not one of them grinned, or nudged his neighbor, or even shifted his eyes away self-consciously. Their faces, in fact, reflected nothing more than varying degrees of disgust. Pete came over and rubbed Cisco's shoulder affectionately. Angel helped me gather up the poly-fiber stuffing, and even Tiffanie, with her bruised and scratched face, volunteered uncertainly, "I've got a sewing kit. I found it last night when you told us to check our packs."

Cisco came over and pushed the rabbit once or twice with his nose, trying to bring it back to life, but even he knew it was too late. I managed a smile for Tiffanie. "Thanks," I said. "I'll check with you tonight when we make camp."

I would have bet everything I owned at that moment that none of the kids had had anything to do with destroying Cisco's toy, which left only the so-called counselors as the prime suspects.

And that was scary.

CHAPTER ELEVEN

The door of the interrogation room opened and a man in a sheriff's department uniform entered. He went straight to Ritchie and bent to whisper something to him. Ritchie listened intently for a moment, and then nodded. I watched anxiously until the uniformed man left.

I said quickly, "Did you find—have they found—?"

"Not yet." His expression was grim. "We knew the search would be slow in these conditions."

"What about the murder weapon?"

"It might be spring before we find it, if then."

I sank back in the chair, trying not to shiver. My coffee was lukewarm, but my throat hurt from talking so long, so I took a sip. It only made me colder.

Agent Brown said, "Why would anyone want to break into your tent, Miss Stockton?"

"That's what I couldn't figure out," I said tiredly. "It's not as though I had anything anyone would want to steal. And then, after I saw what someone had done to the toy, I thought maybe they wanted to hurt Cisco."

"That would be a foolish thing to try."

"Maybe not for a city kid who doesn't know about dogs. Besides, golden retrievers are a lot more friendly and trusting than other breeds. It's not as though he would have tried to defend himself. He would have defended me. But not himself."

Agent Brown said, not unkindly, "And you would have done anything to protect him, wouldn't you?"

I drew a breath to assert that of course I would, I would have protected my dog to the death, and that was when Mr. Willis said calmly, "Let's try to remember that Miss Stockton is not on trial here, gentlemen."

I was beginning to see why it was a good idea to have him here.

There was a moment of silence. I stared at the muddy depths of my coffee cup.

Detective Ritchie said, "So that stuffed toy you were talking about, how did it end up in the wrong hands? Is that what somebody was trying to break into your tent to get?"

I shook my head. "They never even got the flap open. I think Cisco probably dropped it at the camp fire, or somebody took it from him. I don't remember him having it when we went to our tent."

Agent Brown smiled a little. "So that might be what you could call an opportunistic crime, am I right?"

I knew he was trying to lighten the mood and put me at ease again. I refused to respond.

Detective Ritchie said, "You were the only one who packed your own pack, right?"

I nodded. "Except for Rachel and Paul, I guess."

"What kind of weapon did you pack?"

I scowled sharply at him. "None. I didn't pack any weapons."

Agent Brown made a show of checking a page of his notes. "But you do have a carry permit, am I right?"

"Of course. But I don't see what—"

"And on a dangerous excursion into the wilderness for almost a week, you didn't bother to bring a firearm?"

My contempt for the FBI agent was mounting.

Clearly, he wasn't from around here. "Not with a bunch of kids along. And I didn't think we'd be seeing too many rattlesnakes in the middle of January with the temperatures staying close to freezing."

He simply nodded and made another note. "So you didn't have anything in your pack that could qualify as a weapon."

"I had a Swiss army knife," I said. "I kept it zipped in my jacket with my phone and waterproof matches. It's standard survival procedure." Automatically I reached to pat my pockets, as I had done so many times the past few days, but of course they had taken my jacket at the desk. And they knew exactly what was inside the pockets.

Detective Ritchie sipped his coffee, watching me as he said, "What about a hatchet? Isn't that what you'd call a standard piece of survival equipment?"

My throat clenched. "I thought you said you hadn't found the murder weapon."

Ritchie replied mildly, "We haven't."

My attorney spoke up. "Okay, I think it's time for a break. My client is tired. We can pick this up—"

I said firmly, "No, I don't want a break. I want

149

to finish this." I looked sternly at Detective Ritchie. "I didn't have a hatchet. Hatchets are heavy and not worth their weight on a trip like this, at least to me. Paul was the only one who had a hatchet."

Ritchie leaned back in his chair, his sweater-clad chest expanding with a breath. "Okay, then. Let's get back to what happened that morning. This is day two, right? And you're still in North Carolina?"

I nodded. "We'd cross into South Carolina before noon."

Agent Brown made a note. "How do you know this?"

I gave him a dismissive glance. "I have GPS on my phone, remember?"

"Ah yes," he said. "The phone."

"Right." I gazed into my coffee again, contemplated taking a sip, and thought better of it. "The phone."

CHAPTER TWELVE

I wasn't the only one who was looking at my fellow campers with a suspicious eye that morning, and the tension around the cooking fire was palpable. Tiffanie was still pouting about her scratched face, and although Rachel had almost convinced her the fall had been an accident, I wasn't so sure. I had not imagined the half-open zipper of my tent, nor the scrambling shadows when Cisco barked. Why anyone would want to break into my tent—or be foolish enough to try, with an eighty-pound golden retriever sleeping inside—I couldn't begin to guess.

As for the stupid trick with Cisco's rabbit, I thought I was probably being more sanguine about it than most of the kids. Cisco had already forgotten about the rabbit, as he had forgotten about every toy he'd ever had that had ended up being shredded by the Aussies or left in a muddy ditch to rot or had accidently disintegrated in the washing machine. It was the meanness of spirit behind the joke that creeped me out, and I suspect that was what had upset most of the kids, too. One thing they taught us in therapy dog training is that children often identify with dogs, which is why they will tell secrets to a dog that they would not share with a parent, teacher, friend or counselor. I wondered how many of them were remembering a time when they had been unfairly victimized, perhaps even threatened, just as Cisco had been. I wondered how many of them had a secret they would like to share with Cisco.

I packed up my tent and sleeping bag and scooped up some hot water from the communal pot that was simmering over the fire. I added a portion of the water to the dehydrated dog food in Cisco's collapsible bowl, and the rest to the powdered eggs in my camp mug. A few of the kids were trying to choke down oatmeal—without sugar and without salt, which in my opinion was cruel and unusual punishment on a trip like this—and they kept offering Cisco their leftovers, with the best of intentions, I'm sure.

"Cisco is on a special diet," I told them. "People food will make him sick." It's what I always say to people who try to feed my dog. The truth is that, while Cisco does have a few food allergies that have persuaded me to do more cooking for him than I do for myself, I have seen him wolf down pizza, ham sandwiches and coconut cake—to name only a few—with no ill effects.

"Lucky Cisco," Tiffanie said glumly, gazing at the goo in her cup. "This crap is making me sick too."

She watched with interest as I sprinkled chili powder from a foil package over my eggs, and added a full packet of ketchup. "It helps the flavor," I explained, stirring the concoction together. "A lot."

She grimaced. "Where'd you learn that?"

"My dad. He used to take me on overnight hunting trips when I was a kid, and this was our camp breakfast."

Her eyes widened. "Hunting, no kidding? What did you hunt?"

"Deer mostly. Sometimes bear."

At the tortured mixture of dismay and astonishment on her face, I had to grin. "Usually what we hunted them with was a camera. My dad wasn't much of a shot."

She stirred up a spoonful of oatmeal, and let it plop back into her cup. "At least he wanted you with him," she said. "I don't remember my dad ever wanting to take me anywhere."

I didn't know what to say to that. I ate my ketchup-y breakfast in three quick bites, and said, "Listen, Tiffanie, while you were up last night, did you see—"

"Anybody messing around in the woods with that stuffed toy?" Already she was shaking her head. "I wish I had. That's just mean. That's like taking candy from a baby. Or something worse. That's just stupid and mean. If I would've seen them, I would've let them have it, and don't you think I couldn't."

I made up my mind right then and there I would never let it be known that the destruction of Cisco's toy had meant more to them that it would ever mean to him. As far as the kids were concerned, this was a violation, a cause against which they could all unite. And since they appeared to uniting for me, instead of against me, far be it from me to argue with their logic.

I said, "Actually, I was wondering if maybe you noticed anything, you know, out of place. Tent flaps open, somebody moving around…"

She shook her head. "I just went to pee. If anybody'd been watching me, I would've noticed, you can bet your life on that. And then when I got back to camp, there was a lot of noise and confusion, you were there…"

"I was only there after you fell," I reminded her. This is why eye-witness testimony in court is often useless.

She scowled. "Yeah. Right. Anyway, after that everything was a mess. And if you want to know what I think is crazy, did either one of *them…*" She shifted her eyes meaningfully toward Rachel and Paul, who were giving crisp orders to the boys about how to fold up their tents. "…even ask you about what happened this morning? Did they even notice? They're always talking about teachable moments, but, like, did they even care?"

Good point, and one that had not escaped my notice. I said, "You're pretty smart."

Sometimes, a few words of encouragement can change a child's life. Other times it will earn you a fierce, derogatory look and a short, "I got a freakin' 1600 on the SAT, you want to make something out of it?"

By this time Cisco had finished his breakfast, licked the bowl, and was sniffing the ground for remnants. I scraped the last bits of eggs and ketchup from the sides of my cup, swallowed them, and said, "See ya."

She glared at the oatmeal in her cup. "What're we supposed to do with this?"

I dug in my pocket and came up with an extra ketchup packet. "Eat it," I suggested.

After another moment, she tore open the ketchup packet, emptied it over the oatmeal, and actually ate it.

~

I tried to get Heather alone all morning, but whether by accident or design she was always with a student or with Rachel or Paul. I've been around the block once or twice and I've seen the dark side of human nature more than I like to remember. Maybe it has something to do with spending most of my time with dogs, but I do like to imagine the best in people, and I really, really wished I didn't have to think about Heather what I was thinking now.

But why had she lied about Max?

And how had she happened to arrive first at the scene of Tiffanie's accident with her coat already on, when the rest of us—except for Rachel—had stumbled out half-dressed?

The morning was blustery and the sky was

leaden, but the kids were in better spirits than I expected after a night of interrupted sleep and a morning of unsalted oatmeal. We made pretty good time up the winding wooded trail for the first couple of hours, and then I let myself fall behind the others and dialed home.

I knew Maude would just be finishing cleaning the kennels this time of day, so I let the office phone ring. She answered briskly on the fifth ring. After confirming that all was well on both our ends—I saw no reason to worry her with the unpleasantness I had encountered on the trail—I asked her to check my phone records for October. We keep a data base of everyone who calls about any of our services, because our monthly e-mail newsletter is our main form of advertising. You never know when someone who didn't have time to bring his puppy to obedience class will turn out to be a regular grooming client, or vice versa. The only problem was that we had had a fire in mid-October with considerable damage to the office. Back then, I only backed up our files once a week, and I was hoping that Brian's call hadn't come in during that lost period of time.

My spirits sank as she said, "No... no, I don't see anyone by that name on our contact list. Let me check the class schedule. CGC, did you say?"

"Yes, but he never actually showed up."

"Nonetheless, he appears to have filled out a registration form via e-mail. Brian Maddox, mailing address is a Hansonville post office box, telephone area code 216… I don't recognize it. Probably a cell phone."

"Ohio."

A pause while she tapped a few keys, then, "You're right. How do you know that?"

"Lucky guess."

"His dog's name was Kelso. Two-year-old black lab."

"A.K.A. Max," I murmured.

"Well, isn't that interesting?"

"It certainly is."

I thanked Maude and disconnected and, while I still had some privacy, I quickly dialed my uncle at home.

It was a heart attack that had forced Uncle Roe into retirement, and I did not like to bother him with work-related questions. My aunt did not like it when I bothered him with work-related questions, either, and I never would have done so had Buck been in town. On the other hand, "retirement" for my uncle was shaping up to be more of a part-time job, and already he had started to organize a cold case squad from the surrounding mountain counties' sheriff's departments. The chances are that Buck would have referred me to my uncle, even if I had been able to reach him. Brian Maddox's body had been found after Buck took over, but he had disappeared while my uncle was still sheriff. If a report had been made in Hanover County, he would remember it.

My aunt answered the phone and sounded surprised when she heard my voice. "Why, Raine, I thought you said you were going on some kind of hike this week."

"I am," I told her. "I'm in the mountains right now. I'm calling you from my new smartphone."

"Well, isn't that a marvel? You sound clear as a bell."

"I know. It's great. Is everything okay there? How is Majesty?" My aunt had adopted my collie, Majesty—or I should say, Majesty had adopted her—back in the fall, and never had a woman and a dog been more content together. Nonetheless, I missed my girl and couldn't help asking about her.

"Right as rain and snoozing in front of the fire this very minute."

"Lucky dog." I shivered. "Aunt Mart, I need to

ask Uncle Roe something. I wouldn't bother him with this, but you know Buck is on vacation and I just need to know if he remembers anything about a case from last fall."

"Well, he's not here, honey, but if it's important I can have him call you back." Her voice sounded hesitant and a little worried. She added, "Raine, you did hear about Rosalee, didn't you?"

Rosalee Lawson was Buck's mother, my former mother-in-law, retired in Florida now for almost ten years. I got a horrible feeling in the pit of my stomach. "No. Is something wrong? Is that why Buck is in Florida?"

"Honey, she died Friday afternoon. The funeral is Sunday. We sent flowers. I left a message on your home phone, but I figured you already knew."

Crap, I thought, but didn't say that out loud to my aunt. I had been fond of Rosalee, although we hadn't been in touch for years, and I was sorry she was gone. But mostly I felt rotten for the things I had been thinking about Buck, as though it was his fault he wasn't there when I expected him to be. As though his whole life should revolve around my convenience. I said, "Thanks, Aunt Mart. Listen, there's no need for Uncle Roe to call me back. I'll talk to him when I get home."

"Okay, honey. You take care out there, you hear me? And stay warm. The weatherman says snow."

After another moment's hesitation, I dialed Buck's cell phone. It went straight to voice mail, and I was glad. I never know what to say at such moments. Not even to a machine. "Buck, this is Raine. I just heard about your mother, and I don't know what to say. You know I loved her. I'm so sorry. I'm not at home. I'm actually on a wilderness hike, but I just wanted to call and tell you—well, I'm sorry."

I spent the rest of the morning feeling pretty glum—nostalgic and mad at myself, embarrassed for being too quick to jump to erroneous conclusions about Buck, and not at all interested in making conversation. That was just as well, because no one else was either. The weather had taken a downward turn, with an ugly wet look to the clouds and an icy wind from the north. The kids walked with their heads down and their collars pulled up against the wind, too miserable to even complain.

When I did catch up with Heather, it was unintentional. Even though I had not done this in a while, I was still in better shape than the average weekend hiker, and I had Cisco to keep me motivated. I had already passed all the girls, and when I came upon Heather she had paused to rest beside the trail. She had removed her back pack and braced her hands on her knees, stretching out her back. She looked winded.

"Guess I wasn't as prepared for this as I thought," she said when she saw me.

"That makes two of us." I kept my voice casual and friendly and even let Cisco go up to her for a pet. I glanced at the sky. "Any word on when we might be making camp? Looks like we might be getting some weather."

"Talk to Mr. Evans. He's up front. My guess is he's trying to give our day leader a lesson in wise decision making."

I said, still keeping my tone easy, "So, how did you end up with Kelso?"

She went still. Her face lost all expression and she stared at me. "What?"

"Brian Maddox's dog," I explained. "The one you call Max. Are you the one Brian left him with the last time he went on a wilderness hike? The time he didn't come back?"

She said coldly, "I don't know what you're

talking about." She turned to pick up her pack.

"Why did you change his name?" I insisted. "Don't you know the Evanses would have recognized him the minute they saw him?"

She made a derisive sound in her throat. "They don't even recognize the counselors on sight, much less the dogs." I saw a quick flash of alarm in her eyes and realized she had not intended to admit I was right. She tried to hide it with a gruff, "Besides, so what if they did? I haven't done anything wrong."

She shuffled into her backpack, studiously avoiding my gaze, but I wasn't letting her off the hook that easily. "Haven't you?" I replied pleasantly. "What about putting that bottle of booze in Cisco's pack to try to get me fired? You must've been afraid I'd mention to Paul that I recognized the dog. That's a lot of trouble to go to just to keep a secret."

Panic stirred far back in her eyes, but then she lowered her gaze, jerking on the straps of her pack. "I don't know what you're talking about."

I shrugged and edged past her on the trail. "Have it your way."

She grabbed my arm. Now the panic in her eyes was not so vague. "You're not going to say anything, are you? What difference does it make whose dog it is? I didn't steal him!"

I pulled my arm away. "Then why do you care who knows?"

I started to move on, and she said quickly, "It was Rachel who tried to break into your tent last night. When Cisco barked she ran away and pushed Tiffanie down so she wouldn't see her."

I looked her over coolly. "Why would Rachel try to break into my tent?"

She swallowed. "I think… maybe she was trying to get your phone."

"And you know all this," I said, watching her, "because you were hanging around my tent, too— tearing the stuffing out of Cisco's toy rabbit."

A dull flush confirmed the truth. I turned in disgust and started up the trail.

"Listen," she said quickly, "it's not that simple. Give me a chance to explain. Only…" I heard the voices of the girls behind us on the trail, and she cast a quick and frantic look in that direction. "Not now. Please?"

I threw my hands up in a *whatever* gesture and strode past her up the trail. I was so mad that I walked faster than I probably intended, and Cisco was trotting to keep up. I passed Pete, who trudged along a few yards behind Jess. There was no more joking or conversation, and both boys walked with their heads down.

"Maybe it would be a good idea to check the map for a place to take a break," I suggested to Jess when I reached him. "We've been walking a long time."

"No need to check the map," he said. He shrugged out of the straps of his backpack and let it drop to the ground. "Found one." He sat down in the middle of the trail.

That was *not* what I had meant.

"Where's Mr. Evans?" I asked, and he made a vague forward gesture. Pete came up and dropped to the ground beside him. I moved on.

The trail, which had been wide and even in the flats, had narrowed as we climbed, hugging a tall hill on one side and rugged, brambly woods on the other. In some spots there was barely room for two people to walk abreast, and when I caught up with Paul a couple of dozen steps farther down, the trail had grown so twisted that it was impossible to see what lay even six feet ahead. I called out and he waited for me.

"The kids are tired," I said, and noticed my own breathing was a bit labored. "Jess and Pete have staged a sit-in a few yards back down the trail. Will we be taking a break soon?"

He scowled in annoyance. "The trail divides just around that bend. I told Jess we'd take our midday break there. If he would learn to read a map…"

He shouldered past me back down the trail toward Jess. I watched him for a moment, then kept moving along the trail.

As we approached the bend, the trail narrowed to such an extent that Cisco and I could not walk side by side, so I released him to the end of his expandable leash, about eight feet ahead of me. He caught the scent of something and, nose to the ground, urged me forward. I make it a practice never to increase my pace to keep up with my dog, and Cisco knows that pulling will get him nowhere. The reason he knows that is because every time he tries, I stop dead in my tracks and wait for him to return to me. That is exactly what I did when, in his excitement over the new scent, he bounded to the end of his leash. If I hadn't done that, the chances are that this story would have had a very different ending indeed, and I probably would not be the one telling it.

I never saw it coming. One minute Cisco's

white-feathered tail was waving in front of me, the next it was not. I screamed, *"Cisco!"* and dived for him. I hit the ground hard. Dirt sprayed into my mouth, I clawed at rocks. Fingernails ripped. I could see his startled eyes, surrounded by white, and his paws scrabbling for purchase on the edge of the cliff. I grabbed for his collar and clutched only a handful of fur. He started to slip. I screamed again.

"Cisco!"

CHAPTER THIRTEEN

They say your life flashes before your eyes. But when you love a dog, the *future* flashes before your eyes: a future without him. It was only an instant, but it was an instant of a big black abyss—a future with no waggy golden tails, no happy panting grins, no golden paws scrambling across my wooden floors and dashing across my lawn and leaving big muddy paw prints on my porch. And then, in the next breath, he was licking my face, digging his claws into my thigh, panting into my ear. I wrapped my arms around him, shaking, my face buried in his fur, breathing in his warm, doggy scent with my whole being.

"Are you okay? What happened?"

"Yo, dog! Hey, man!"

"Whoa, guys!"

I yelled, "Stay back!" I flung out a hand in the direction of the voices and Paul and Jess, followed closely by Pete, came to an abrupt halt. I said, breathing hard, "We're okay; it's okay. The trail is out. Stay back."

Paul extended his hand to me and I grasped his forearm, pulling myself up. I held Cisco close by the collar and we edged ourselves back onto the solid part of the trail. Paul's expression was grim. "You're off the trail," he said. "How did you miss the sign?"

I stared at him. "What sign?"

Paul turned to the boys with an abrupt gesture. "Okay, guys, move back. This area is off-limits. Jess, get out your map and get us back on the trail."

The boys turned back reluctantly and, I must say, I thought they showed a good deal more concern about what had almost happened to Cisco and me than the so-called adult in the situation did. In fact, anger sparked in Paul's eyes and his tone was clipped as he turned back to me. "Miss Stockton, we cannot have this. You presented yourself to me as a trained professional with wilderness experience. I have my hands full taking care of the students in my charge. If you can't take care of yourself, or at least manage to keep yourself out of harm's way, you're a liability I simply can't afford."

Oh, there were a lot of things I could have said, most of them at the top of my lungs and peppered with four-letter words. But I'm a dog trainer, remember? I know that animals, when frightened, will often express fear as anger and usually turn on the one least equipped to fight back. Humans are as much animals as dogs are and are subject to the same instincts. The worst thing you can do in the face of irrational anger is to react with anger yourself.

So I said calmly, "Cisco, with me." And I moved around Paul, back down the trail, until I reached a point where we could stand side by side. "What sign?" I repeated.

In retrospect, of course, I could see exactly where the trail ended: at the point where a sheer bluff protruded onto the flats and narrowed the trail into a mere sliver of a footpath that curved out over the ravine and then abruptly stopped. There was no way you could know it stopped without edging around that bluff, however, and by the time you did that, it would most likely be too late. All things considered, it was a good thing that Cisco, with four feet and a superb since of balance, had gone first, and not one of the kids.

Paul looked around, scowling, took a few steps down the trail, came back. And then he swore softly and pointed at the leaf-covered drop-off about twenty feet below us, where a wooden sign with the word "Danger" stenciled on it in orange letters lay discarded in the rubble.

"The wind must have blown it down," he said. There was no trace of an apology in his tone. "We'll have to make sure it's replaced." He turned away from me and called, "Jess, how're you coming with that map?"

It was possible, I suppose, that the wind might have blown the sign over. It was even possible that it might have blown the sign off the trail and down the ravine. But if Paul had looked a little closer he would have noticed what was very obvious to me: two symmetrical holes in the ground, the fresh dirt still dark with winter damp, where something had been pulled straight up out of the ground very recently. Something like a sign.

I couldn't entirely repress a shudder as I knelt down to hug Cisco one more time. But the great thing about dogs is that they live almost entirely in the present, and Cisco, now with all four paws once again safely on terra firma, was grinning happily and ready to move on. We went to join the others just as Heather and Angel came up, followed closely by Tiffanie.

"Doofus here got us off the trail," Pete was explaining to them irritably. "Now we've got to go all the way back and figure out where he screwed up."

"I didn't do any such thing! We're on the damn trail!" He thrust a half-crumpled trail map in Pete's face. "See for yourself!"

Pete swiped the paper away. "You don't even know how to read that thing!"

"Like you do!"

The mistake they made (and, if I was completely honest, the one that Cisco and I had also made, although not entirely on our own) was one that was common to a lot of rookie hikers. Mountain trails don't always go forward. Sometimes they actually go *up*—as in up the vertical embankment and over the rocks where, I could see from where I stood, the footpath picked up again on the fairly level terrain about five feet over our heads. The boys, not anticipating this, were still looking for a place that the trail might have forked without their noticing.

Naturally, I opened my mouth to point this out, but I caught the warning in Paul's eye and closed it again. Apparently, this was some sort of test. I only hoped they figured it out before Lourdes and Rachel caught up with us and made the same mistake Cisco almost had. I was getting pretty sick of these tests, and as a note for future expeditions: the wilderness is *not* the place to test your hiking savvy. Take an online course. Practice in a nice safe national park. Don't bring a bunch of kids out into God's Country and expect them to prove themselves or die. For crying out loud.

"Look at your map again, Jess," Paul advised calmly. "The route is clearly marked."

"I looked at it! It says we're right where we're supposed to be!"

Heather said, gesturing forward, "What's up ahead?"

Jess held out his arm in a staying motion. "Dead man's bluff," he said. "Doggie dude almost bought it."

Heather's eyes flew to me in alarm. "Oh my God! Are you okay?"

I gave what I hoped was a nonchalant shrug. Inside I was fuming. "Close call," I admitted. "We just need to make sure no one goes past this point."

Paul said nothing, and Jess, glowering, turned back to study the map. Pete pushed past him impatiently, marching back down the trail in the way he had come. "You missed a turn, you dope. It's got to be back here somewhere."

"Hey, wait a minute." Frowning, Jess looked up

from the map, looked up over his head, and I knew he had figured it out. He followed Pete until he spotted the access point. "This way, man."

Though the climb was short and there were handholds, it was not, by any stretch of the imagination, suitable for the inexperienced hiker. Jess made it up, but only by stripping off his pack and leaving it with Pete. When he realized the only way to get his pack up the wall was with a rope, he had to climb back down to get it. After that things went more smoothly. Cisco was in high spirits and ready for anything, but there was no way I was going to send him up that bluff until I checked it out myself. Pete scaled the cliff and hauled his backpack over the edge, and I was right behind him, leaving Cisco with Tiffanie. I pulled my backpack over the rim, then instructed Tiffanie to loop the rope through the ring on Cisco's backpack.

The boys had been too busy congratulating themselves on their success to even notice when I scaled the wall, much less offer to help, but they wandered over curiously when I called down to Tiffanie, "Okay, when I say, give him a push."

She hooked her fingers beneath Cisco's collar and called back, "Ready!"

"Cisco," I commanded, "scramble!"

I tugged on the rope at the same moment Tiffanie boosted Cisco up the wall, and the boys watched in fascination as Cisco scrambled up the wall and over the edge. Jess even reached down to help him over, and Pete helped me with the rope. To Cisco it really wasn't that much different from the A-Frame on an agility course, but for the boys it was a chance to put their lessons in teamwork into practice, and they laughed with pleasure in their success when Cisco put four paws on the ground again.

"Way to go, little dude!" Jess ruffled Cisco's fur companionably, grinning.

"How'd he learn to do that?" Pete wanted to know.

While I was explaining about Cisco's training, Rachel and Lourdes arrived, and I suggested things might go faster if we pulled up the backpacks while the girls were climbing. Before they knew it, we had an assembly line going, with Pete hauling up the backpacks, and Jess helping the girls over the edge. Kids, like dogs, almost always do better when they have a job.

Paul was the last one over the edge, and announced we had reached our day two campsite.

The kids were ecstatic—or at least, they were

what passed for ecstatic under the circumstances. They had marched a torturous trail for four hours and had climbed a wall, literally, and they deserved a break. The bluff was wide and flat, and the ground was a bed of pine straw. Setting up camp was easy. The wind was miserable, though, and I made sure the kids dug an extra-deep pit for the campfire. In conditions like those, a single spark can take out a forest.

The tents were set up and they had a small fire going when I saw Heather walk away from the campsite, presumably in search of more firewood. I handed Cisco's leash to Lourdes. "Keep an eye on him for me, will you? I'll be right back."

Her jaw dropped open, but her hands closed around the leash. "Me? You want me to watch him?"

"Sure," I said. "Why not?"

Tiffanie came forward, reaching for the leash. "I'll do it."

Lourdes hands tightened on the leash defensively. "She said me."

"It's fine." I ran a protective finger under Cisco's collar and smiled at Lourdes. "Just don't choke him okay?"

I followed Heather into the woods.

I was raised by a mother who did her best to make me into a Southern lady. I'll admit I've been in a fistfight or two in my life. But they were mostly with boys, and to be honest those boys had a severe disadvantage: they had been raised by the same kind of mother I had, who taught one unbreachable rule—never hit a girl. Nonetheless, as I marched toward Heather McBane, I had never in my life wanted to punch a girl in the face more than I wanted to punch her. I was practically trembling with the effort to restrain myself when I caught up with her.

"We could have been killed!" I said to her, low and hard. My hands were clenched into fists in my coat pockets. "You pulled up that sign and tossed it over the cliff. Cisco was tied to me! If he hadn't been, he would've fallen to the bottom of the ravine. If I hadn't been paying attention, we both would've fallen! Are you crazy? What in the name of all holy hell were you thinking?"

There was genuine panic in her eyes, and a hint of terror. "I'm so sorry! I never meant to hurt Cisco! I didn't know—I didn't think you would be the first—I didn't know!"

I grabbed her shoulder. "Who?" I practically screamed at her. "Who were you trying to hurt?"

She wrenched away from me, breathing hard, her eyes wounded and wild. "Don't judge me! You don't know what's going on here! You don't have any idea! You seriously *don't have any idea.*"

I tried to look rational. "Yeah, okay, well tell me about it, Heather. Tell me what it is I don't get. Because I am about thirty seconds away from turning you into Paul, or the police, or whoever it takes to get your crazy ass off this mountain and away from these kids who don't deserve to have their lives put in danger by your crazy-ass, irrational, *stupid* agenda, whatever the hell it is. So talk."

Okay, a little over the top. A little too many crazy-asses. I briefly cursed the mother who had made it a crime in my mind to hit a girl. I thought about Cisco going over the edge of the cliff, and the wild panic in his eyes when he realized there was nothing but air under his feet and I wanted to punch her. I really, really did.

"I didn't mean to hurt anybody," she said, but the way she slid her eyes away told me that wasn't exactly the truth.

I took a step toward her, my fists clenched in my pockets. One more step and I would be guilty of assault.

Her gaze flew to mine, and it was filled with a pathetic mixture of anxiety and remorse—and maybe, because she was not entirely stupid, just a little fear. "I didn't mean for anyone to get hurt, really. But Paul always goes first, he knows the trail and I thought he'd see—"

"Jess was in front," I told her tightly. "You knew that!"

"He never lets the kids go first! He pretends to but... I didn't mean for anyone to fall!" she insisted desperately. "I just figured if enough things went wrong, some of the parents would demand an investigation, and then they'd find out..."

"Find out what?"

She wiped a nervous hand across her face. "What's really going on. Who—what—he really is. That's all I want."

But I was at that moment less concerned with who Paul really was than whom Heather really was. Pieces of the puzzle were falling through my brain like snowflakes that melted on contact and it took me a long, frustrating moment before I could put my hand around a solid clue. "Wait a minute," I said, staring at her closely. "You told me this was your first time out. That you hadn't been on this trail before. How did you know about the dead spot in the trail? How did you know where the sign was?"

She licked her lips. She avoided my eyes. "That's not important," she said. "What's important is—"

"Oh my God," I said softly. "That's where he died, isn't it? That bluff is where Brian Maddox fell."

She said harshly, "He didn't fall."

I stared at her.

She cast her eyes quickly around and took a step closer, as though afraid of being overheard. She spoke low and fast. "I tried to tell the police, but these local yokels wouldn't listen to me. They just wanted the whole thing off their books. Brian called me right before he died. We were on video chat just minutes—I think just minutes before he was killed." Her voice choked a little here, and she bit her lip briefly. She continued in a stronger voice, "He had proof of what was going on here. Paul found out about it and Brian was afraid to stay here. He left the hike the second day to get the evidence back to the authorities and then all of a sudden, what do you know? He's dead. I came out last fall with his parents to identify the body, and I made the rescue people take me to where he was found. That's how I knew about the bluff."

"What kind of evidence?" I demanded. "Evidence of what?"

The wind whipped her hair across her face and she pushed it back impatiently. "They were shut down a couple of years ago in Ohio when they were accused of child abuse. They beat the charge because the kids were too scared to testify. It's not just sexual abuse. It's sexual humiliation. Torture. Threats. Psychological battery. That's what Paul Evans gets off on. That's how he controls them."

I felt queasy. "If that's true, someone would have come forward. These programs are pretty tightly regulated—"

"Didn't you hear me?" she practically screamed it at me. "These kids are victims of terrorism! He has them so scared not one of them would risk testifying against him. I know, because I talked to some of the kids who were in Brian's group. I knew what they had been through. I told them I knew. And they were like survivors of a Nazi prison camp. They got hysterical when I even mentioned this place. Talk about scared straight." She gave a short bark of humorless laughter.

"But their parents—"

A brief, angry shake of her head. "They're in

denial, most of them. They wanted an easy fix and they got it. They're busy, important people. They don't have time for details. Some of them, a few of them, suspected something was wrong about this place but didn't want to dig too deep. Their kids were off drugs, out of the bad habits, obedient and respectful, and they could get on with their lives. That's all they wanted."

She took a breath. "Brian was a journalism major, and he was interning at a local television station when he came across the story and found out they had just changed their name and moved to North Carolina. He thought if he could get in as a counselor, he could find out what was really going on. And he did. He said he had video on his phone of Paul with some of the kids that would break the story wide open. He tried to e-mail it to me but it wouldn't go through from here. Like I said, he was trying to get away from them, and we were on video-chat, when he said he heard someone coming. The last thing he said to me was, 'They can't get their hands on the phone. I'm going to hide it.'" Her expression was bleak. "I knew by the next day when I hadn't heard from him that whoever was following him had caught up with him."

A gust of wind made the overhead branches groan, and we both hunched our shoulders against it. I said, trying to keep my teeth from chattering, "And you told this to the police?"

She nodded, "They said there was no evidence that anyone besides Brian had left the camp. But people leave camp all the time, you know that, and unless it's one of the kids, no one notices."

I pointed out carefully, "Anyone could have missed the trail in the dark, or even in full daylight. There's no reason to assume—"

"You sound just like the police! Brian was an experienced hiker. He had done the Andes and Nepal and the freakin' Appalachian Trail twice, okay? He did *not* just fall off a bluff in the dark. Not unless he was running from someone, and even if he had, it wouldn't have killed him. Not like that. The coroner's report said the cause of death was a blow to the head and they assumed it was from the fall. But that ravine was all brambles and branches; there weren't any rocks. He might have broken a leg from the fall—or even his neck—but he wouldn't have fractured his skull."

I had certainly heard less compelling arguments, but I knew nothing she had said would stand up in court, or even persuade a medical examiner to re-open the case. I said, "So you were Brian's girlfriend? The one he left Max—I mean, Kelso—with while he was here?"

She nodded. "He called me every day. I knew something was wrong when I didn't hear from him, but as far as everyone else was concerned, he wasn't even due back for two weeks."

"What about the video?"

She shook her head. "They never found his phone. Brian said he was going to hide it, and he did. But they found his backpack almost fifty yards up the trail from where they found him."

I frowned a little. "That's odd." I really couldn't think of a good reason why an experienced hiker— as Heather had claimed Brian was—would abandon his pack. Even if he was running from something, or someone, you don't ditch your lifeline. Of course, if someone had taken it from him...

She thrust her hands into her coat pockets and turned abruptly. "We shouldn't stay here. They'll get suspicious."

I said carefully, "About what?"

The look she tossed me was filled with anger and disdain, but also with a discernible measure of fear. "You don't have any idea," she said, "what they're capable of. What they've already done. What's at stake. I'm sorry you got involved. I'm just... sorry."

And with her hands balled in the pockets of her coat, her head down and her shoulders bowed against the wind, she walked rapidly back to camp.

There was no point in calling her back. I wouldn't have known what to say. I didn't even know what to think. Because it has become almost instinctive to me to dial the sheriff's department when I have a problem of this nature, I reached automatically for my phone. I had four messages from Melanie.

There was no point in calling Buck. Even if he had been back at work, I would not have known what to say to him. I thought about calling Uncle Roe. I called Melanie instead.

"Where have you been?" she demanded petulantly when she answered.

I was cold and tired and had bigger things preying on my mind, and I might have been a little short as I replied, "On top of a mountain, freezing my..." A quick edit. "Fingers off. I told you I couldn't keep my phone on."

"Well, you need to come get Pepper. Right now."

This was not a video call. Nonetheless, I took the phone away from my ear and stared at it in disbelief. There was even a note of laughter in my voice as I replied, "What?" because I couldn't believe she was serious.

"Right now!" she repeated shrilly. "I mean it!"

I could hear the tears in her voice, and the surprised amusement I had felt died immediately. "Melanie, what's wrong?"

"She's a terrible puppy! She peed herself three times today and Grandma made me wash her in the laundry tub. And then I had to wash her bed in the washing machine and as soon as I put it back in her crate she peed on it again. I took her outside for *two hours...*" I was pretty sure that was an exaggeration. "And as soon as I brought her in again she peed right on the floor! She's a horrible puppy and I hate her! I don't want her anymore!"

I had not had a great day, and my voice was a little more stern than it probably should have been. "Well, too bad for you. You made a commitment, remember? Puppies are a lot of work. You don't just give up on them when the going gets tough, and you can't just give them back."

"Why not?" she shot back. Her voice was wet and angry. "That's what my mother did to me!"

I squeezed my eyes shut, cringing at my own stupidity, and blew out a long slow breath. There is a reason why I have dogs and not children. Dogs are so much harder to screw up.

I said, "Listen, Melanie, your dad is coming home pretty soon, right?"

"No!" She sniffed noisily. "He's got things to do and I'm not supposed to call him at work. Well, I've got things to do, too. I have to go to school, don't I? And I've got to do my homework, don't I? I can't do everything!"

And although it felt as though someone was wringing out my heart like a dishtowel when she said that, I tried to focus on the problem, and I kept my voice calm. I thought I knew what had happened. "I'm sure your dad didn't mean you couldn't call him. He's your dad. Of course he wants to talk to you. But in the meantime, you know Pepper is just a puppy. Did you forget to tell Grandma how often to take her out? You can't leave her in the crate all day while you're at school and then get mad when she has an accident. It's not her fault. But it's not your fault either. Puppies have accidents. You have to be patient." I paused and added gently. "Do you miss your dad?"

"No!" She sniffed again. "I don't care if he ever

comes home." And then, in a muffled tone, "I don't really hate Pepper. I love her. I'm sorry I said you should take her back."

"I know. Sometimes it's hard when you have to be in charge of everything."

She sniffed again, loudly. "Sure is."

"But I know you can take care of Pepper. She depends on you, and you're not going to let her down. But you don't have to do it all by yourself. Tell Grandma to call the dog walker, okay? Everything's going to be fine."

When I was Melanie's age, my dad used to let me go to court with him, and to sit behind the bench with him between cases while he signed papers. I felt like queen of the world sitting up there, looking out over the courtroom with my dad in his long black robes. Sometimes he would let me hold his gavel, and because I understood exactly how significant that responsibility was, I always took it seriously. I felt important, sitting up there on the bench with my important dad. I felt needed. But most of all I felt loved.

I dialed Miles's cell.

I hadn't bothered with the video, but I could tell by his voice this was not a good time. "Hey, babe. I'm in a meeting. I'll call you back."

"No, you will not." I was cold and tired and at the end of my patience with parents who had better things to do than take care of their children... and children who had better things to do than take care of their puppies. "What you'll *do* is get on a plane and go home and take care of your daughter!"

"Mel?" His tone changed immediately. "What's wrong? Is she hurt?"

"She's alone and scared and she needs her daddy, that's what's wrong. You have a child now, Miles. You're responsible for her, and I'm not her mother! She barely even knows me! You can't just take off for God knows where whenever the mood strikes you and—and leave her in her crate like you would a puppy. Kids need more than that. So do puppies!"

I was a little incoherent, I know. I had been through a lot in the past few hours.

He said, "Hold on." There were some muffled sounds, during which I assumed he left whatever meeting he was in, and then he said, "Damn it, Raine, make sense. I talked to my mother two hours ago. Melanie was fine."

"She is not fine! Her mother abandoned her and now so did you."

"I did nothing of the sort. She knows—"

"She thinks she can't even call you when you're at work. For crying out loud, what kind of father doesn't take his children's calls? Tom Cruise will shut down a movie to take a call from one of his kids, did you know that?"

There was a brief silence. "My phone is always on." His tone was subdued. "Melanie knows she can reach me."

"She shouldn't have to! You should be with her. When I was a little girl—"

"Damn it, Raine, this is not the eighties! We're in the middle of a global recession and I'm trying to save my business, do you mind? In the meantime I don't need you telling me how to raise my daughter."

"Well, someone needs to! She is not going to grow up like this, Miles! She's better than that, and she deserves better than that, and five years from now you're not going to be sending her to a place like this just because you didn't do your job!"

"What place? What job? What are you talking about?"

"You know perfectly well what I'm talking about. Having a child is a commitment, got that? And you don't get to just walk away when it gets hard."

"Are we still talking about Melanie?"

If I had been in the mood to pay attention, I might have discovered he had something perceptive to say, but even if I had given him a chance to speak, I probably wouldn't have listened. So I snapped back, "That's the trouble with the world, you know that?"

"What?"

I returned shortly, "You!" and disconnected.

CHAPTER FOURTEEN

The morning of the third day dawned with a brilliant red sky, which as any sailor—or wilderness hiker—knows, is not a good sign. I pointed this out to Paul, who was using his hatchet to slice off the bottom branches of a poplar to build up the fire, and he agreed without much appearance of concern. Snow is a fact of life in winter camping and can even add a little glamour to the experience. Of course that usually wears off after the first few hours of searching for dry firewood, which is why I always carry a camp stove.

"We might have to weather a day or two at the lodge if snow moves in," he said. "We've got extra provisions there. No problem. Why don't you do your search and rescue demo this morning, and we should have plenty of time to get across the gorge by afternoon. One more night under the stars. Or clouds, as the case may be." He gave me a friendly, if impersonal smile, and moved past me with an armload of wood.

I picked up a few fallen branches and followed, hurrying until I drew even with him. I said, "This is where they found Brian Maddox's body, isn't it?"

The shock on his face was not unexpected, and he slowed his pace, staring at me. "How could you possibly know that?"

Before I could think of an answer, he found one for himself, and it made him frown. "Oh, right. You're in the search and rescue business."

"Also in the police business." I didn't think it would hurt to remind him of that. "Or at least my family is."

The frown only deepened, but I couldn't tell whether it was from anger or concern. "That was a tragedy. I was lucky we were able to keep the New Day name out of it. Brian was a hot-headed kid and what happened was his own fault. He wasn't even technically employed by us when he died."

He glanced around the clearing and muttered uncomfortably, "I didn't realize this was the place." He looked at me sternly. "I'll trust you to keep this to yourself. There's no need to upset the students or disrespect the dead."

If he was lying, he was good at it. But then

again, I didn't consider myself a particularly good judge of character.

~

I ate another quick pre-packaged meal and, while Cisco was gobbling down his, I turned my back to the crowd around the campfire and quickly texted Melanie.

Everything ok?

Seconds later the phone blinked in my hand.

Great! Dad is coming home today!

Well, good for him. At least he knew when to take a hint. I have to admit, I felt a surge of smug satisfaction and I started to text her back when I heard Paul's voice behind me. I quickly turned the phone off.

"Miss Stockton, the sooner you get your demo set up the sooner we can get back on the trail."

I knelt in front of my backpack, which I had been in the process of packing for the day, and casually slipped the phone into a pocket with my camp cup and wet wipes. "Almost ready," I called back.

Melanie was okay, I had absolutely no desire to talk to Miles, and with everything else that happened that day, I didn't even think about the phone again.

Until it was too late, of course.

~

The morning was bitter and damp, the air thick with unborn snowflakes. The kids relaxed around the fire while I explained how I had started training Cisco as a puppy by playing hide-and-seek and how I taught him to track and retrieve objects by smearing them with peanut butter. They liked that, which lead to a brief digression in my speech to explain the long and lauded role that peanut butter has played in training canine stars from Lassie to the latest Westminster champion. I'm good at this, but even if I weren't, it's hard to fail when you have good material. The kids were rapt.

Heather volunteered to hide herself in the woods a few hundred yards away while I moved on to the specifics of search and rescue techniques and training. I wasn't too thrilled with either the choice of victim or the choice of terrain, since I knew that area of woods was crisscrossed with human scent, and Heather's in particular, from the day before. That meant it would probably take Cisco longer than usual to search the terrain, so I told her to wrap up in a space blanket to stay warm and to cover herself with leaves for disguise. I wanted the search to be enough of a challenge to be impressive, but I didn't want to spend more than ten or twenty minutes on it. As much as the kids were enjoying the break in the routine, that was how much I didn't like the look of the sky. I wanted to get to the next camp site before the snow started.

"Cisco is trained to follow human scent," I told them, concluding my speech on the complexities of scent pooling and the rigors of training a search team. "He should pick up the freshest trail automatically. This is why, as I explained to you earlier, a good scent dog doesn't necessarily need a target object—that's something that was recently handled or worn by the person he's tracking—to pick up the trail." All of this was a bit optimistic, I admit. Cisco was an enthusiastic, but easily distracted tracker. More than once in tracking class, he had sent me on a merry chase through the woods in search of a deer or a rabbit. His find rate was good, but he was young and still training.

"However, since there have been a lot of people

through the woods this morning, we're going to give Cisco an advantage by letting him get the scent of Heather's glove." I took out the glove-liner that Heather had left with me earlier, and let Cisco sniff it. Of course, what he really wanted to do was to play tug with it, and I quickly put it away. "Okay." I snapped Cisco's long line onto his backpack ring. "Let's see how long it takes Cisco to find Heather. Remember, his signal for a find is to sit and bark. And don't forget to stay behind me, otherwise you'll contaminate the trail."

"What if he can't find her?" Angel wanted to know.

"Then I'll be embarrassed," I admitted, and she giggled a little.

"Ms. McBane has her whistle," Rachel said humorlessly. "And if it takes too long, we'll blow a whistle to let her know the exercise is over."

I bent down and brushed the ground with my hand. "Cisco, track," I said.

He took off in a happy crisscrossing pattern, his nose to the ground, moving in what I was pleased to note was the right general direction.

"So do you, like, track criminals and stuff?" Pete asked.

"Sometimes. But Cisco is not a police dog.

Mostly we find lost people."

"Why do you keep the rope on him?" asked someone else. "In the movies, the dogs search by themselves."

"Some dogs work better off-leash," I said, not entirely dodging the question. "Cisco doesn't."

Fortunately, the terrain was fairly flat and clear, so that the line did not become snarled as it would have done in a more heavily wooded environment. We had arranged in advance that the search would take us in the general direction of our destination, so that, even though we left the trail after a few dozen yards and spread out in the woods, we really weren't losing much of the day's hiking time.

I started explaining to the kids about search grids, and the kind of role they each might play if this were a real search mission, and then, to my dismay, Cisco started excitedly sniffing a half-rotted tree stump. Suddenly he sat, and barked.

"Hey," exclaimed Lourdes. "That means he found something."

Jess gave her a derogatory look. "Yeah, well unless she's the size of a squirrel, there's no way she's hiding in that stump."

I held out an arm as they started to move past me. "No, Jess is right," I said. "Don't contaminate the trail."

Paul drew up beside me. "It looks to me as though the trail is already contaminated," he said dryly.

I was embarrassed, just as I had predicted. This wasn't anywhere near the place we'd agreed on for Heather to hide. I said, still trying to sound in control, "Dogs are not fool-proof. Sometimes they get confused by other things in the field, or by the tracks of other people. I'll check it out."

I walked up to Cisco and brushed the ground again. "Cisco," I repeated sternly, "Track."

But Cisco remained stubbornly sitting, waiting for me to reward him for a good find. Once again, he barked.

On more than one occasion, I had come to regret second-guessing my dog. Cisco might occasionally get over-excited and forget a command or two, and he had once or twice been known to forget his mission altogether, but he had never deliberately made a mistake about a find. I looked around more closely, wondering if Heather might have dropped a glove or even a tissue on her way past. And that was when I noticed it. Wedged inside a corner of the stump, half-covered by damp leaves, was a blue waterproof bag, the kind campers use to store soap and writing materials and other small items in. I pulled it out. It was battered and stained and looked as though it had been there awhile. And there was something inside.

I raised the bag to my nose. It smelled suspiciously like peanut butter.

Cisco barked again.

I quickly reached in my pack and took out his tug toy. "Good find!" I exclaimed, tossing it to him. "Good find, Cisco!"

Cisco caught the toy in midair and did a happy twirl, and that was apparently a single to the others that our demo was over. They all crowded around.

"Hey, what's that?"

"I thought he was going to find a person, not a bag."

"Maybe there's cash inside."

I opened the drawstring and pulled out exactly what I expected to find: a cellular phone. It was a lot like mine in size and shape, maybe one model older, and looking a little worse for wear. I pushed the power button, but of course the battery was long since dead.

Somebody said, "Say, whose is that?"

I remember that Rachel was standing on one

side of me, and Paul on the other. Rachel said nothing. Paul reached for the phone. "Let me see that."

I ignored him. I turned the device over and saw a small address sticker there. A lot of people do that, in case they leave their phone on an airplane or in a cab. I guess it's more common in cities than around here. The sticker, which was faded and peeling at the edges, read:

*Return to Brian Maddox * 451 Candlewick Lane #12* Pendleton, Ohio 43780.*

Paul withdrew his hand as though it had been about to touch a ghost. "Good God. Is that...?"

"Looks like some camper lost his phone," I said, clearly enough so that I wouldn't have to repeat myself to the kids. "I'll turn it in to the police when we get back."

I dropped the phone and the bag into my backpack and zipped the pocket, watching Paul all the time. Well, what was he going to do, argue with me?

Maybe he would have liked to, but all he said was a brusque, "All right, Miss Stockton, that was certainly very interesting, but I'm afraid we can't waste any more time on this demonstration. Rachel, call Miss McBane in. We should get back on the trail."

Rachel gave several sharp blows on her whistle, and after a few moments Heather caught up with us, brushing the leaves from her stocking cap and adjusting her own pack. "What's up?" she wanted to know. "You didn't even give him enough time to find me."

"He found something better," Jess said. "A telephone. Maybe he can call us all a cab."

The laughter masked Heather's reaction as she stared at me. "Whose?" she demanded, pretending to be shocked. "Whose phone?"

I wasn't about to get into it with her there, and because both Rachel and Paul were still within hearing distance, as well as a couple of the kids, I said casually, "Some guy from Ohio. I'm going to turn it over to the police when we get back."

Paul said loudly, "All right, everyone, back on the trail. We've wasted enough time."

Pete muttered, "Thanks a lot, pooch. We were supposed to have the morning off."

"It wasn't his fault," Lourdes said shortly. "He found something, didn't he?"

"Look at Lard-Ass kissing up to the pooch," Pete jeered. He made kissing noises and lunged toward Cisco playfully, but Lourdes caught his shoulder and jerked him back.

"Hey, cut it out!" he said, wrenching away from her angrily.

"You cut it out!"

"Both of you cut it out," I said impatiently. I certainly had more important things on my mind, and I was annoyed because Heather had already moved away without giving me a chance to say anything further to her, or to gauge her reaction while I did. "Cisco, with me." I drew Cisco close and bent to replace his tracking line with his hiking leash.

"Besides, everybody knows it was you that cut up the pooch's toy," Pete said meanly. "No point in trying to make it up to him now."

I looked up in surprise, and Lourdes face was dark red, her eyes blazing, her fists clenched. "I did not! You liar! You know you're a liar! Take it back. Take it back right now!"

"Hey," I cautioned, but my voice was quickly drowned out.

"I will not! You're the only one crazy enough to do something like that—"

Lourdes hauled off and hit him in the face with her fist. Pete stumbled backward and went down. Cisco started to bark. Before I could stop her,

Lourdes charged at Pete again and got in another blow before I was able to tumble forward and grab the strap of her backpack while, almost at the same moment, Paul grabbed her opposite arm and pulled her off of Pete roughly.

"What is the meaning of this?" he demanded, eyes furious.

"Crazy bitch! Crazy bitch!" Pete pushed himself to his feet, brushing off his clothes and rubbing his cheek, while the others crowded around. He wasn't bleeding, but he would definitely have a black eye. "Did you see that? She just jumped me! Crazy bitch!"

Lourdes yelled at him, "I'll do again, you stupid liar!"

I stroked Cisco's head, trying to calm him, but he was panting and pulling at the leash, eager to get in on the action. "There was some name-calling," I explained to Paul. "Things got a little out of hand. I think if everybody just calms down…"

Paul turned to Lourdes, his expression ice-cold and full of quiet contempt. "That's it, Lourdes. Twenty points."

Her face drained of color. "But—you can't do that!"

"You know the penalty for fighting."

A slow and awful terror filled her eyes. "That means I can't go home. I was supposed to go home after this. You promised I could go home! You can't make me stay. You can't do that—you promised!"

She moved toward him and he took a quick step back, flinging up a hand in self-defense. The alarm I saw flash in his eyes was almost instantly replaced by contempt. "I can do whatever I want, young lady," he said. The way he looked at her actually gave me a chill.

Then, as though suddenly aware that I was watching him, he hitched up the straps of his backpack and turned abruptly. "Back on the trail," he announced loudly. "Jess, get these people moving. Are you leading this hike or not?"

Everyone had grown very quiet and uncomfortable, and as they shuffled back toward the trail, they avoided looking at Lourdes, as though her misfortune might be contagious. Lourdes herself just stood looking stunned and white with shiny tear tracks cutting through the dirt on her face. And then, with a lurch, she pushed forward in line after the others.

"I don't understand," I said. "What did he mean about points?"

Heather was examining Pete's bruised face, but

when I spoke he jerked away and moved on without answering. He looked almost as miserable as Lourdes.

Heather explained, "The program works on the demerit system. Everybody starts out with a hundred points, and that's how many you have to have to graduate. You lose points for things like swearing, disobedience, disrespecting other students and counselors, and you can earn them by following the rules, keeping your quarters clean, doing your chores, that sort of thing." I could tell she wanted to add an opinion about the system, but because Rachel was nearby she added only, "Everybody gets twenty points for completing the hike. There are no more chances to earn points. Lourdes needed every one of them to graduate from the program. Her evaluation will probably recommend another six weeks at New Day." Her voice was tight, but she managed to keep her expression neutral as she glanced over at Rachel. "Is that right, Mrs. Evans?"

"It's not appropriate to speculate on a student's progress with an outsider, Miss McBane," Rachel said. "Go and walk with Lourdes on the trail. Make sure she doesn't get into any more trouble."

"It wasn't her fault," I said to Rachel as Heather

obediently moved off. "Pete was teasing her. Everyone is tired. If you ask me—"

"No one is," she replied shortly and pushed ahead, leaving me to bring up the rear—alone.

A few minutes later, it started to snow. I thought the day couldn't get any worse.

I was wrong.

CHAPTER FIFTEEN

Detective Ritchie said, "So you're telling us that after an extensive search of that same area by trained officers—including canines—that lasted almost a week and failed to turn up anything, that your dog found Brian Maddox's phone hidden in that tree stump in what? Ten minutes? And this after it had been there for four months?"

"Of course not," I replied wearily. "Cisco went straight to the scent he had been told to find—Heather McBane's. And it didn't hurt that she had spruced it up with a little peanut butter. She obviously hid it there on her way to conceal herself for the demo. If Cisco hadn't found it, she knew we'd all come back that way and she could pretend to find it herself."

"Why would she do that?"

I shrugged. "You'd have to ask her. Maybe to

spook Paul and Rachel. Maybe to see if they could be spooked. I don't know."

"Did Miss McBane tell you how she came to be in possession of the phone?"

"She had spent all of the autumn searching the trail. Remember, she was on video chat with Brian when he said he was going to hide the phone. She might have recognized some landmarks."

"If the phone contained evidence like she said, why wouldn't she just turn it over to police?"

"Because it didn't contain evidence. After all this time, even in a protective bag, the circuits were shot. Have you been able to get anything from it?"

Ritchie glanced at Agent Brown, then gave an almost indiscernible shrug of conciliation. "Not yet."

Agent Brown searched among his papers until he found a topographical map of Angel Head mountain. "Can you show us the approximate area where you found the phone?"

I studied the map until I got my bearings and pointed out the site. "We were still in North Carolina."

"And what time did you reach the gorge?"

I thought about that. "A couple of hours. The snow slowed us down, not because it was thick, but because it was something different and the kids were distracted. In a way I guess that was a good thing. The mood was pretty bleak after the scene with Lourdes, but after awhile it picked up again—for everyone but Lourdes, that is."

Detective Ritchie said, "You mentioned the hatchet. Did you see what Mr. Evans did with it after he used it to cut firewood that morning?"

"No. I assume—"

"You've answered the question," my attorney reminded me gently, but firmly.

"So you didn't use it yourself after he did, maybe to go back and get more firewood?"

"No." This time I kept it brief. My throat was starting to hurt from talking, anyway, and I still had a lot more to say.

"Would you be surprised if we found your fingerprints on it, then?"

"I'd be surprised if you found anyone's fingerprints on it," I returned with an impatient scowl. "The temperature never got above twenty the whole day. Everyone was wearing gloves."

I could see the lawyer was trying not to smile. "My client will be happy to supply a set of elimination fingerprints, of course."

Agent Brown turned a page on his notepad. "So

you're now in South Carolina, is that right?"

"That's right."

"You weren't too happy when you saw the bridge, were you?"

Mr. Willis said sharply to me, "Don't answer that."

Agent Brown persisted, "Didn't you have a big fight with Paul Evans there on the edge of the gorge?"

The door opened just then and a female voice chorused with Mr. Willis's. "Don't answer that."

I twisted in my chair. "Sonny!"

She unwound a cable-knit scarf and removed the smart felt hat that covered her long silver braid as she came into the room. The men got to their feet, because Sonny had that effect on people, and she plucked off a glove and extended her hand first to Ritchie and then to Agent Brown, announcing briskly, "Sonny Brightwell, Ms. Stockton's attorney. I'm sorry to be late." She nodded to Mr. Willis. "Bryson, thanks for your help. Raine, do you need anything?"

I could have cried, and from nothing more than the joy of seeing a familiar face. "Oh, Sonny, I can't believe you came all this way! How did you get here so fast?"

She smiled at me, shrugging out of her coat. "It pays to have friends with private planes," she replied and took the empty chair beside me. "Are you okay?" Her hand, still cold from the outdoors, closed over mine. "Is there anything I can get for you?"

"Cisco," I blurted. I sounded a little desperate, but I knew she would understand. "Can you check on Cisco? They told me some vet has him and he hates the vet. I don't want him to stay there. Can't you—"

"The best thing you can do for Cisco is to finish up this interview and get out of here," Sonny told me firmly, and though I knew she was right, her response chilled me. Usually Sonny would have some quip about what Cisco was thinking or feeling; her empathy with animals, although I often made fun of it, was one of the main reasons we were friends. Her brusque, lawyerly demeanor made me think I was in bigger trouble than I had imagined.

She sat back and flipped open her briefcase. "Bryson, is there anything I should know?"

"We seem to be right on track," the other lawyer assured her and passed a couple of papers across the table to her.

Agent Brown looked at me sourly. "For an innocent bystander, you certainly do have a high-class legal team."

I of course opened my mouth to protest, but Sonny simply smiled pleasantly at him. "Thank you, sir," she said. "I always try my best to be high-class. Could we get some fresh coffee in here?"

Detective Ritchie went to the door and spoke to someone, then resumed his seat. "Now if everyone is settled..." He glanced around the room with an exaggerated expression of politeness. "Let's pick up where we left off. What happened when you got to the bridge?"

I stared at the oily black remnants of coffee in my cup and saw my own pale features reflected there. I swallowed hard. It was still hard to think about the bridge. But the story was almost done. I had to go on.

So I did.

CHAPTER SIXTEEN

A couple of inches of snow had accumulated on the trail by the time we reached the gorge, less in places where the ground was leafy or shaded by trees. It frosted Cisco's coat and rimed my wool hat, but it wasn't so bothersome as to obscure vision or obliterate the trail. At this point it was hard to tell whether this was going to be a real weather event, or just one of those pretty snowfalls that blows away by morning. These kinds of snows are pretty typical of the winter weather we get in the mountains, so I didn't see anything to be particularly worried about. For a while the snow even made the temperatures feel warmer, and I'll take snow on a hike over rain any day.

Heather and Lourdes were just ahead of me

for most of the hike. I could tell Heather was speaking quietly to Lourdes in her counselor voice, but I couldn't hear what she was saying. I stayed far enough behind, in fact, so that I did not *have* to hear what she was saying, because the next time I spoke with Heather I wanted privacy. Cisco and I were therefore the last ones to arrive at the bridge. The kids had slipped off their backpacks and were taking advantage of the short break to limber up their shoulders and have a quick snack. I placed my pack and Cisco's on the ground beside the others, shook the snow off my cap, and took stock of our surroundings.

The gorge was only about fifteen feet wide, a relatively narrow fissure in the earth in terms of the gorges we have in this part of the country, but it was at least thirty feet deep, lined with sharp rock shelves and spiky winter-dead trees. It was spanned by a rope-and-slat suspension bridge that would have been risky to cross under ideal circumstances. Under no circumstances would I attempt to take Cisco across.

I looked around until I spotted a footpath to the bottom of the gorge, and another one ascending the opposite side. Whoever had built the footbridge had used the paths to cross the gorge, and the metal handholds they had used for guides were still in place. The path was steep and hard to see, and I knew that the longer we waited the more risky it would become.

Paul had gathered everyone around and was lecturing them on safety procedures while crossing the bridge. I edged my way through the kids to stand beside him, and interrupted him in mid-sentence by closing my hand around his jacketed arm. He glared at me, but the snow was coming down harder now, and there was no time to waste.

"There's a footpath that's safer," I said, gesturing. "But it won't be for much longer." I swiped a hand across my face, clearing my eyelashes of snow. "This bridge is already starting to ice up and who knows how old that rope is? I wouldn't trust it under these conditions."

His eyes were as cold as the leaden sky overhead, and at least as unforgiving. "I didn't ask for your opinion, Miss Stockton."

"Yes, you did," I insisted, "when you hired me. That footbridge is not safe."

"I'm the one who decides what's safe, and in my opinion the bridge is safer than the path. We've trained for the bridge and the program will not be complete without it." He looked from me to Cisco with disdain. Cisco shook the snow from his coat and returned his gaze pleasantly. "If your dog can't make it, leave him behind."

I gave one incredulous shout of laughter and turned away. "Maybe Cisco and I should leave *you* behind," I tossed back, and it was such a childish thing to say that even I was embarrassed by it. I added grudgingly, "We'll be waiting on the other side. Cisco, let's go."

That was when I realized that everyone had been listening to our exchange. Their faces were red and chapped and their lips cracked with cold, their eyes dark and scared-looking. "Hey," Jess said worriedly, "you're not really leaving are you?"

And Tiffanie added, "He can't really make you leave your dog here." But her brows were drawn together and she actually looked uncertain.

"Get your packs on!" Paul called behind me. "Jess, you're in the lead."

Heather cast an uneasy glance toward the bridge, "Do you really think it's unsafe?"

Rachel said loudly, "You heard Mr. Evans! Get your packs! Line up behind Jess."

But Jess didn't move. Neither did anyone else.

I looked from one scared, half-frozen face to the other. There was nothing particularly safe about taking a slippery, rocky footpath down into the gorge and back up the other side, either, and if I had had my preference I would have camped here until the weather cleared. But with the lodge on the other side of the gorge only a few hours away, staying here in the elements did not make sense either. "Look," I said. "Cisco and I are taking the path. It's longer and harder. Anyone who wants to come with us is welcome to."

Paul shoved in front of me, glaring over the group. "Anyone," he said distinctly, "who refuses to cross that bridge will not graduate from the program. Are we clear?"

There was a rumble of outrage, but he shouted over it. "Are we clear?"

A gust of wind flew down from the mountain peaks at that moment that almost knocked me off my feet. The hood of my coat blew up around my face and Cisco staggered and squinted his eyes against it. The rope bridge canted at a forty-five degree angle before swinging back the other way. When I saw it my heart dropped to my stomach, but not as drastically as it dropped when I saw the sudden flash of terror on the young faces before me. On the one hand, they were convinced they would die on that bridge, and I have to admit I'd done my share to contribute to that impression. On the other hand, they faced a fate worse than death for many of them—that of being forced to stay in the New Day program another six weeks.

The northern blast died down and was countered by a lesser gust from the west. Rachel stepped forward in a way that could not be construed as anything else than threatening. Each word was spoken loudly over the wind, and with over-emphasis. "Get. Your. Packs."

The kids started to scramble toward their packs. I turned to Rachel. "Listen, I'm not kidding," I said urgently. "In this wind the bridge isn't stable. You can't—"

She said fiercely, "I think you've caused enough trouble. If you're not going to help, get out of the way."

Another gust of wind caused her to clutch her hat around her ears and duck her head while her hair lashed across her face. Over the sound of it, Paul shouted, "In line! Now!"

At this point there was a lot of confusion. The kids were trying to sort out their packs, Paul was shouting orders and, yes, I think I shouted back at him. It was stupid. The kids were already scared, the bridge was icy, the wind was kicking up; it was a disaster waiting to happen. All I wanted him to do was to consider some options. But the more insistent I became, the more obdurate he was. And suddenly a clear, shrill voice cut through the noise.

"Stop it!" Lourdes screamed. "Stop it, everyone!"

Several heads turned toward Lourdes, including mine, although I couldn't see much through the crowd. Paul ignored her.

"Jess," he barked, stepping onto the bridge, "Let's go."

"You don't have to!" Lourdes pushed forward, her face scarlet and her cap and hair frosted with snow. She held something up in her clenched fist, but I couldn't tell what it was at first. Her eyes were a dark blaze that chilled even me when I looked at them.

"I've got nothing to lose," she said, shoving through the others. Her eyes were fixed on Paul. "I'm not taking it anymore. And the rest of you don't have to either."

Paul gave her a single dismissive look. "Get your pack on, Lourdes, or we'll leave you behind. Talk is cheap, surviving a winter storm in the middle of the wilderness by yourself is another matter altogether. You know I'll do it. Fall in."

She responded lowly, "Fall in yourself, you son of a bitch. It's over."

For a moment no one said anything. Paul stared her down. I was too astonished to move, and so, I think, was Rachel. Oddly, it was Angel who moved forward, putting herself between Lourdes and Paul, and said, obviously uncomfortable, "Come on, Lourdes, you're only making it worse. Move back."

Heather stared to move forward, and I could see a hint of panic in her eyes. "Lourdes…"

But Lourdes whirled on them all, her expression wild and furious, and she held up the object in her hand like a talisman, high for all to see. It was a smartphone. "Listen to me!" she cried. "We don't have to do this anymore! I have proof! I have proof that will put him in jail! You don't have to do this!"

Paul took a step toward her, scowling.

"What's in your hand? Where did you get that?"

Lourdes was breathing hard, her face dark red and voice hoarse. She locked eyes with Angel. "I used to hate you. I used to hate all of you, because you knew what he was doing to me and you made it worse. But then I realized it wasn't just me."

I saw a creeping stain of horror inch its way across Angel's face and into her eyes, and Lourdes lowered her voice with tight emotion, staring her down. "The so-called strip searches, the cold showers with him watching, the other things… it wasn't just me." And her eyes suddenly swept the group as she demanded. "Was it?"

The shock and shame of truth that flashed across each of those young faces made me sick to my stomach. It was only an instant before anger and denial covered it, but it was there. Then Jess took a step back and muttered, "You crazy bitch. You don't know what you're talking about."

No one else moved.

Lourdes declared triumphantly, "Well, guess what? It wasn't just us, either! This has been going on for a long time and I've got the video to prove it. This kid named Brian taped it all on his phone, but they killed him before he could get it to the police. He hid the evidence though, and this is it. It was his phone Cisco found this morning. The proof is here and now he's going to pay." She turned to Paul and shouted, "Did you hear that, you sick bastard? You're going to pay and nothing you can do will save your sorry ass now!"

Rachel said in a low, harsh tone, "You lied to me."

At first I was confused because I thought she was talking to Lourdes, but then I saw that her gaze was directed at Paul. Her face was frost white and pinched, and in her eyes was as much hatred as I have ever seen one human being direct toward another. She said, "You told me it was just that one time. You said it would never happen again. But you lied and you got caught. You killed that boy! You know you did! It's on you, all of it!"

Paul shouted angrily, "Shut up! You don't know what you're talking about, either one of you! Give me that!"

He lunged at Lourdes and wrested the phone away from her, and after that everything seemed to happen at once. Lourdes screamed and Rachel cried, "You're not going to do this! Not this time!" Paul turned back to the bridge and Lourdes lurched after him. Rachel caught his arm and he wrenched away. He was struggling with her when he stepped on the bridge. Lourdes grabbed at both of them, and Paul drew back his arm and threw the phone into the gorge. The bridge swayed violently. Someone shouted, "Hey!" and one of the girls screamed. Cisco barked excitedly. I never heard a sound from Paul.

I did not have a clear view of what happened. I saw Lourdes stumble back, her eyes wide and terrified. Rachel fell to one knee, desperately clinging to the guide wire of the wildly bucking bridge, her mouth twisted into a silent oval of horror as she stared into the chasm below.

Paul was gone.

~

It was all so surreal that for a moment I did not even understand what had happened. And then Angel began to keen, "Oh my God, oh my God." And Lourdes gasped in a strange, high voice, "He fell. He fell. He just fell."

Suddenly my legs were moving, but it might have been because Cisco was pulling me forward. I shouted, "Cisco, halt!"

Dogs live almost entirely on an emotional level. Under any other circumstances Cisco might very well have ignored me, but the raw terror in my voice must have penetrated even his own hyper-excited state and he locked his legs. I unsnapped his lead, commanding, "Down." Cisco sank reluctantly to his belly, his alert and anxious gaze taking in every move as I hurried to the edge of the gorge and looked down.

My breath stopped in my throat as I saw Paul's crumpled form tangled amidst the snow-covered brush on a rocky ledge about ten feet below. The snow was coming down in thick fast flakes now and there was no way to tell how badly he was hurt, or if he was even still alive. I called, "Paul!" But I barely had enough breath to be heard over the sound of the wind. So I tried again, stronger now. "Paul! Can you hear me?"

I thought I heard a faint answering moan and saw a small movement of his arm in reply. I looked at Rachel, who was still kneeling at the edge of the bridge, clutching the wire. "He's alive," I said. I called over my shoulder. "He's alive! Someone get my phone out of my pack and call 911!" I reached for Rachel's arm, urging her to her feet and back to safety. "It's okay. It's going to be okay."

Lourdes was crying and Angel and Tiffanie were on their knees beside her with their arms around her, crying too. Cisco held his down stay, looking so anxious to be of help that he was practically quivering. The boys stood close together, stunned into silence. Heather was just turning away from my backpack, and I directed her breathlessly, "Tell them we need an airlift, and if they can't get Life Flight, a forest service copter will do. I'll go down and see how badly he's hurt, but we can't leave him there in the cold. We've got to have help. "

Heather was not dialing, she was not speaking. She just stood with her back to me, staring at the phone. She turned slowly, the expression on her face weak and sick. She had a blue camp bag in one hand and a battered Smartphone in the other. She held both of them up to me wordlessly.

For a moment I didn't understand. "Lourdes got the wrong phone," Heather said dully. "This is Brian's phone. Yours went over the cliff."

And that's when everything changed.

CHAPTER SEVENTEEN

I looked up anxiously when the door opened again, but it was only a deputy with a pot of coffee. There was a slight relaxation of tension while cups were refilled and packets of sugar and artificial creamer dispensed. The deputy had brought a folder with papers in it, and I assumed they were statements from some of the other kids. Agent Brown and Detective Ritchie passed them back and forth. Sonny asked if I wanted to take a break. I shook my head.

Agent Brown leaned back and sipped his coffee, glancing over his notes. "So help me get a picture of this. How many people were actually on the bridge when Mr. Evans went over?"

"I don't know for sure." I was trying to be a good witness. I knew how important accuracy was. But I now also understood what strange tricks the mind could play when a person was in the very center of a crisis. I honestly had no clear recollection of the details of that moment. "Rachel must have been on the bridge, because that's where I found her when I reached it. I don't know whether Lourdes was on the bridge or at the edge of it. Paul couldn't have been more than a foot or two on the bridge when he went over, which is why he hit the slope instead of falling into the chasm."

"And how far away from the bridge were you?"

I thought about that. "Maybe three or four feet."

"Close enough to reach it in one step?"

Mr. Willis said mildly, "Answered." And Sonny added, "What part of 'four feet away' did you not understand, Mr. Brown?"

He looked annoyed. "That's Special Agent Brown, Miss Brightwell."

Sonny just smiled.

Detective Ritchie said, "Yet you couldn't see what was happening on the bridge just…" He pretended to consult his notes. "Three or four feet away from you."

"Maybe it was farther than that. I didn't want Cisco too close to the edge."

He nodded. "Did anyone else approach the bridge while Paul Evans was on it?"

"No. Just Lourdes."

"And would you say that Mrs. Evans seemed surprised by Lourdes's accusations?"

I tasted my coffee. It was rich and hot and tasted freshly made. I felt my spirits revive a little. "Surprised, maybe. More like angry at her husband."

"Was there a struggle on the bridge after Mr. Evans threw your phone away?"

I shook my head. "I couldn't tell. There was a lot of yelling and Cisco was barking, and I must have looked away for a second to try to calm him down."

"What did you think had happened to Paul Evans?"

"The wind was kicking up. The bridge was icy. I assumed he overbalanced when he threw my phone, and he fell off the bridge."

"Evans didn't scream when he fell?"

"No."

"But Lourdes did."

I thought about that. "Someone did."

"Could he have been pushed?"

Sonny said impatiently, "Anything is possible, Detective. My client has already told you she didn't see what happened."

231

Detective Ritchie nodded noncommittally. "What would you say was Rachel Evans's state of mind at this point?"

"She was in shock, I guess. To tell the truth, I didn't pay much attention to her state of mind. I had too many other things to worry about."

"Was she crying?"

"No."

"Did she offer to help when you went down the cliff to check on her husband?"

"No."

"What about the other kids? I guess they were pretty upset by it all."

I nodded. "They were at first. But they got themselves together. They remembered their training." I could feel the gamut of emotions flicker across my face: horror, disappointment, outrage, but at last, pride and triumph, as though I had actually been in some way responsible for their final performance out there. Which I suppose I was. "There were some rough moments," I admitted. "But in the end they proved what they were made of. They did what they were supposed to. They're good kids, down deep, and they'd been through a lot. I don't blame them for what happened."

Agent Brown's expression was unimpressed.

"What was your state of mind when you realized Paul Evans had fallen, Miss Stockton?"

That seemed like a stupid question. I should have known by then to beware of stupid questions.

"I was upset, of course. Just like everyone else. I couldn't believe it. I was afraid he was seriously—maybe even mortally—injured, and I didn't know how we were going to get him to a hospital in time. These kinds of rescues are hard enough with a qualified team of medics and good weather. I was scared," I admitted. "I was afraid the outcome might not be good."

"And when you realized that Evans had tossed your phone—your only chance to get help, not only for him but for you and all those kids—how did you feel then?"

"I couldn't believe it at first. I had to look at the phone Heather had found and make sure it was Brian's. Then I tried to turn it on, but of course the battery had died months ago. Then I searched my backpack, hoping there had somehow been a mistake, but there hadn't been."

"You must've really been scared then," Ritchie said. "And pissed."

I said, "I was alarmed at first. But then I remembered Paul had a phone and I figured we

233

would use it to call for help as soon as I could get to it."

"So why didn't you?"

I took another sip of my coffee to lubricate a suddenly dry throat. "His phone was in his coat pocket. It was smashed on impact."

Ritchie nodded sympathetically. "And then what did you think?"

I stared at him incredulously. "What do you mean, what did I think? I was hanging by a rope off the side of an icy cliff in a blizzard with an injured man, five kids, two women and my dog depending on me and no way to get them to safety! I thought I was in trouble, that's what I thought!"

Sonny placed a calming hand on mine, and I took another sip of coffee.

Agent Brown said, "How did you get to Mr. Evans?"

"I tied a rope to a tree and rappelled down. It wasn't very far. I could have climbed the slope if it hadn't been so slippery. The snow was really coming down, and by the time I reached Paul, he was almost completely covered."

"But he was alive?"

I nodded, swallowing another gulp of hot coffee. "His leg was broken, and probably some ribs. He had a lot of superficial lacerations and the bleeding made them look worse than they were. He was in an awful lot of pain and kind of floating in and out of consciousness. I used an inflatable splint from my emergency pack to stabilize his leg, but I didn't really have enough room to work so I probably didn't do a very good job. I gave him some codeine tablets, wrapped him in a couple of blankets, and tried to figure out how we were going to get him out of there."

Ritchie asked, "Why didn't you just lift him back up to the top of the cliff? You had the ropes, and you said it was less than ten feet."

I nodded slowly. "That would have been the best plan. It wouldn't have been easy, but I think we could have done it."

"Why didn't you?"

I couldn't reply at first. I was silent for so long that both Mr. Willis and Sonny looked at me curiously, and Agent Brown prompted, "Miss Stockton?"

"I couldn't," I answered. "I couldn't do it by myself, and the kids—they refused to help me." I met Detective Ritchie's eyes. "They wanted to leave him there."

CHAPTER EIGHTEEN

When I reached the top of the cliff, both Jess and Pete were there to grab my jacket, my arms, and the last few inches of my rope harness to pull me over the edge. The snow was blowing like a white curtain whipping back and forth in front of a foggy windowpane, and the wind had the sound of a roaring ocean. Cisco came wagging toward me with tail held low but face smiling, his way of saying that, while he had missed me terribly and was glad I was back, he understood this was no time for exuberant greetings. I hugged his neck, and for a moment, I just clung to his snow-heavy coat, getting my breath.

"Okay," I said, raising my voice to be heard above the wind. I pushed to my feet and began to untangle myself from the rope harness. "The good news is, Paul is alive. The bad news is, his phone is not. We're going to have to make a rope travois— that's like a stretcher—and pull him back up over the cliff. We'll have to hurry before the slope ices up so badly I can't get back down there. I need you guys to get me the ropes from your backpacks— hurry!"

Pete and Jess, who had been helping me unwind the ropes from my ankles, glanced at each other, and stood up. As one, they backed away.

"Come on, guys, I'm not kidding!" The snow was so thick now I actually thought I would choke on it as I yelled at them. I gestured wildly. "Look around you! This is serious weather! We don't have time to waste!"

Jess and Pete, stony-faced, said nothing and did not move.

I stared at them for a moment in disbelief and then shoved passed them, stumbling toward the pile of backpacks that were already half-covered with snow. I grabbed loops of rope from each one and, slipping and sliding, made my way back toward the cliff.

"This is not a game, kids!" I shouted at them. "I need help!" I looked from one to the other of them, my arms sagging with the weight of the ropes and my feet stumbling in the snow. "You're going to have to form a team to lift him up, and I'll need someone to go over the cliff with me to help form the travois." I met nothing but deliberately blank faces and gazes that shifted from mine. I turned frantically to Rachel. "You!" I commanded. "Come with me. I'll help you over the edge. Come on, there's no time to waste, I can't do this by myself!"

Rachel's eyes were as cold as the bottom of an arctic lake. I thought she had not understood me. I screamed, "He'll die!"

She said simply, "Good." And she walked away from me.

I looked through the heavy veil of snow to Angel, Lourdes, Tiffanie, Jess and Pete. They stood like soldiers with their chins set, their hands in their pockets, their eyes averted. Cisco stood watching us all, his anxious breath steaming the air.

I stumbled to Heather and grabbed her arm. "This is your fault!" I screamed at her. "You set Lourdes up! You told her about Brian and you planted that phone!"

She jerked her arm away angrily. "I told her the truth! Someone had to know it! Okay, so I planted the phone but I spent three months combing these mountains to find it."

"You should have turned it into the police! What were you thinking?"

"The police don't care!" she screamed back at me. "They already proved that! So I wanted witnesses, and I found them, didn't I? He's not going to get away with it this time, he's not!"

I could hardly believe what I was hearing. "If he dies, you'll be a murderer!" I was in a panic; I didn't know what I was saying. I said it anyway. "It will be your fault as surely as if you'd pushed him off that bridge!"

The wind whipped her hair across her face and obscured her expression. She may have shouted something at me, but I didn't hear it. I turned away from her, dragging the ropes, pushing against the driving snow. I turned to face the kids. Cisco pressed his snow-covered shoulder against my knee. I dug my fingers into his fur briefly and then braced myself. I raised my voice to such a pitch that I thought my voice-box must be bleeding, and still the wind tore away my words.

"Listen to me!" I pleaded. I looked from Jess to Pete to Lourdes to Angel and Tiffanie. "I don't care who you are, I don't care what you've done. I'm so sorry for what's happened to you here, and if I have anything to do with it, someone will pay, but right now don't you see you're letting him win? If you let him die you are no better than he is, don't you see that? You let him win! Maybe you think this is the right thing to do, the easy way out, but in the end you are the ones who will pay for it for the rest of your lives—with nightmares, with guilt, with regret. Please don't let that happen to you! Haven't you paid enough? You are more than this. I know you are! Please!"

The air was white between us, and faces were hard to see. But no one spoke, no one came forward to help me. I swung toward Rachel and grabbed her arm. "He's your husband!" I cried.

She pulled away, her face filled with contempt. Her eyes were so dead and cold that they chilled me to my soul.

In the few moments I had stood there, a crust of snow had formed on my hat that was so heavy I could feel it, and the strands of hair that escaped around my face were wet and frozen. When I looked down at my boots, I saw they were already covered with snow, and when I looked up at the sky it was bruised and angry, spinning out a brutal vortex of snow that looked as though it could suck us all up into its fathomless core if we weren't careful. If we didn't get moving.

I looked around until I found a sturdy tree and I began to wind a loop around it that was strong enough to hold my weight. When I had secured it, I trudged back to Rachel, shouting against the wind. "The bridge is too dangerous to cross, but you've got to get the kids to the lodge before dark. Can you find the footpath?"

She stared at me as though she couldn't hear me. Frantically, I whirled toward Heather. "I'm going to try to lower Paul to the bottom!" I yelled at her. "Can you get the kids down the footpath?"

Shielding her eyes against the stinging snow, she searched for the path.

A gust of wind almost knocked me off my feet and I could feel time running out. I unsnapped Cisco's leash from my waist and hooked one end of it to his collar. I handed the other end to Lourdes. She looked at me with big questioning eyes as her hands closed around the leash. "When you get to the bottom, let Cisco lead. He'll find me." I turned to Heather. "You'll have to tie yourselves together or you won't be able to see in the snow. Heather, can you do this?"

She nodded numbly. I had to believe that she could. I had no choice.

I knelt and took Cisco's face in my hands. His fur was crisp with snow, and his eyes had a similar look to that I had seen in Lourdes': confusion, uncertainty, but ultimately trust. I pressed my forehead against his for one breath, tightening my fingers in the fur on the side of his neck, and then I stood.

"Go on," I yelled at them, gesturing toward the footpath. "I'll meet you at the bottom."

My plan was pieced together from scraps and desperation. Clearly, it would take less physical strength to lower Paul the remaining fifteen or twenty feet to the bottom of the gorge than it would require to raise him over the ledge, and I thought I could do it myself using the ropes as pulleys. I would have to climb back down to him, fasten him to a rope harness, then scale the cliff again and secure the harness to a tree as leverage so that I could lower him to the next secure ledge. I would then have to climb back down, resecure the ropes, and repeat the procedure until he reached the bottom. It would not be a pleasant journey for the injured man. In fact, the chances of us both making it to the bottom alive were not good at all. But if I left him there, he would surely die.

I was just starting to lower myself over the ledge when Jess grabbed my arm. I was startled. The snow was so thick by this time that I could barely make out shapes within it, and I could only assume—and hope—that the others had followed my instructions and started for the footpath. "I sent Pete with the girls," he shouted to me. The wind half-closed his eyes and tried to snatch his words away. He staggered against it. "What do you want me to do?"

I was too relieved to argue with him. Of course under ordinary circumstances I would have never endangered the life of a sixteen-year-old, no matter how badly I needed his help. But I think we both knew that, whether he stayed with me or went with the others, all of our lives were in danger at that point. And I needed his help. Desperately.

"I'll go down and fasten the harness," I called back. "When it's done I'll pull on the rope twice and you'll lower us both down. Just keep tension in the rope when you feed out the slack. When I get to the bottom, I'll tie off the rope and you can use it to guide yourself down. Be sure to use a safety harness that's secure on this end. I'll show you how."

"It's okay!" he shouted against the wind. "We learned rappelling in wilderness training!"

I wondered if he understood, as I did, the irony of the fact that the man who, only moments ago he had been willing to leave to die had taught him the thing that would now save his life. Both of their lives.

He nodded and I caught his shoulder. I was trusting this kid with my life and I wanted to see his eyes when he answered my question. "Why are you doing this?"

His lips compressed briefly and in the blowing snow it was impossible to read what he was thinking. "Not for him," he returned briefly and turned to get to work.

It took what seemed like hours, working the wet ropes in the icy wind, and by this time, Paul was so delirious with pain that he was no help whatsoever. His leg had begun to swell against the splint and I was worried about cutting off the circulation. He had to have medical attention. But first we had to get him off the cliff.

When the harness was secure, I wrapped Paul's hands around the rope and I shouted to him, "Paul, listen to me. We're going to lower you to the bottom of the gorge. You've got to try to hold on. Use your other leg if you can to keep from hitting the cliff wall. I know it's going to hurt. I'm sorry. Just please try to hold on."

His face was grey and a faint line of frozen saliva rimmed his lips. There was no way of telling from his dull, feverish eyes whether he understood me. But he did tighten his hands around the rope.

I don't remember much about the descent. I did my best to guide Paul down, but even under good conditions it would have been a tricky operation. At one point I lost my footing and if I hadn't been tied to Paul we both would have fallen. At another point a gust of wind combined with a slippery foothold slammed us both against a rock wall. I heard Paul scream with pain, and he lost consciousness for a while. My back and my legs and my arms were numb when we reached the tangle of brush and scrub pine at the bottom of the slope, and Paul was going into shock. All I could do was to cover him with a space blanket to keep the snow off and hurry to help Jess.

Under no natural law should any of us have survived that trip down the slope. An injured man with no one but a woman half his size to keep him from tumbling into the abyss, a teenage boy with no practical rappelling experience, a blizzard in which we could neither see where we were going or hear each other's shouted instructions. At one point I thought I saw Jess swing away from the mountainside and then slam back into it, and my heart stopped. But he righted himself again and completed the descent with nothing more than a torn jacket and a smear of frozen blood on his face to account for the adventure.

I think I knew then that we had no chance of making it back up the other side of the ravine and reaching the lodge before dark. It would have been suicide even to attempt to find the footpath under these conditions. We were stuck at the bottom of a gorge in the midst of a blizzard with no way out and no way to call for help.

I turned my back to the wind and pulled Jess close, shouting into his ear to be heard. "Start putting up Paul's tent," I told him. "Double-stake it. Get inside with him and stay there. I'll find the others."

He shouted back, "Never separate from your group!"

He was right, of course he was. The worst thing you can do in a wilderness crisis is to move, and that's true whether you've just wandered off a hiking trail or survived a plane crash in the Andes. You stay put and let the rescuers come to you. But my dog was out there, not to mention six other people for whom I was responsible, and all of our survival supplies. If I left Jess and Paul, there was no guarantee that I was not leaving them to their death. If I did not leave them, I might never see Cisco again. I knew what I had to do. I just didn't know if I had the courage to do it.

Fortunately, I never had a chance to find out. Just as I was drawing a breath of icy air to speak, I heard a sound so faintly in the distance that I might have thought I'd imagined it had I not seen a flair of recognition in Jess's eyes at the same moment. Torn by the wind and smothered by snow, it was nonetheless unmistakable: it was the sound of a dog's joyful barking.

~

They came out of the sea of snow like a foggy apparition, and I held my breath until I counted six figures, plus Cisco, staggering toward me. Cisco pulled free of Lourdes and barreled into me, happily licking the ice from my face before he shook off his own snow-sodden coat. Heather was dragging the weight of my backpack, plus her own. At least she had sense enough to realize that we'd need the survival supplies in my pack, as well as in Jess's, and they'd all taken turns carrying both. As difficult as it must have been, they had made it down the slippery footpath with only a few scrapes and bumps, and all supplies intact.

I let Cisco go with one last hug and addressed Rachel, "Paul is safe," I told her, "but I think he's going into shock. We've got to get him out of this weather. We're not going to be able to make it back to the top of the gorge tonight. I'll help you set up his tent."

She shouted back over the wind, "You do it!" She shrugged out of her backpack and began to unpack her own tent.

I stared at her. Regardless of her feelings about her husband, regardless of her callous disregard for the injured man, she was still technically the leader of this expedition. She should have given the kids their orders for making camp, their safety plan, the reassurance that she did, indeed, know how to get them through the night. Instead, she simply started beating down the snow for her tent site, ignoring us.

Frantically, I beckoned the others to come in close. They huddled near me with frosty, frightened faces and shoulders tightened bravely against the cold, straining to hear what I had to say. "Okay," I said, "work in two-man teams. Set up all the tents in a circle, no more than two feet apart.

Double stake all the tents. Brush the snow off your clothes before you go inside. Get in your sleeping bags and stay there. Take a bottle of water with you to keep it from freezing. Don't leave your tents for anything, do you hear me? Not for anything!"

I don't know how long it took. The gorge provided some shelter from the wind, but sudden sweeping gusts threatened to snatch the tent canvas out of our hands, sent snow driving into our eyes, and upended unsecured corners before we could drive the stakes into the frozen ground. I erected Paul's tent by myself, got him wrapped in his sleeping bag, and made him as comfortable as possible with water and more codeine tablets. I left my camp stove running to bring up the temperature inside, though I knew there wasn't enough fuel for the whole night. "I'm sorry," I told him, feeling helpless to do more. "We'll try to get help for you as soon as we can, but there's a storm and we have to camp for the night. Try to rest. I'm leaving some protein bars and water here."

I placed the food and water within easy reach and as I was turning to leave, he suddenly plucked at my sleeve. "Listen to me," he said hoarsely, through dry, cracked lips. "It was Rachel who went after the Maddox boy. She heard him threaten me with the video... New Day was everything to her. It was Rachel."

For a moment I just stared at him. Too much was spinning in my brain for me to even process the information, much less make a reply. A gust of wind tore across the fabric of the tent, rocking it a little. I said, "I'll check on you later."

When I crawled out of Paul's tent, someone had put my tent up and secured Cisco inside. He was anxious to be out with the others, but I put him in a down-stay and used the blunt end of Paul's hatchet to make sure the stakes were driven as deeply into the ground as possible on both the tents. I helped Heather get her tent up and passed the hatchet to her while I went to help the girls. When Tiffanie's tent was up, Heather used the hatchet to pound the stakes, and then gave it to one of the boys. Everyone was helping everyone else and no one was asking questions. I lost track of the hatchet.

When I got everyone inside their tents with final instructions not to unzip their tent flaps for anything during the night, I made my way to Paul's tent and checked on him one last time. He was restless and in a lot of pain, but he was breathing normally and had almost stopped shivering.

I brushed off my clothes and my boots as best I could and zipped myself inside my tent with Cisco. Every muscle in my body was heavy and numb, and my chest hurt with the effort to breathe. I rubbed Cisco down with a chamois, taking care to pluck the ice balls from between his toe pads, and gave him food and water. I put on two pairs of dry wool socks and drank some water, then called Cisco to me and zippered us both inside the sleeping bag.

I thought I'd spend hours listening to the roar of wind and the pelting snow, but the next thing I knew I opened my eyes to a strangely quiet blue light. I had vague memories of disjointed dreams that were punctuated by the gunshot-like *crack* of falling trees and the scream of the wind: running the Iditarod with a team of golden retrievers, Cisco and I escaping from a gang of armed teenagers on cross-country skis, that sort of thing. For the most part I was too exhausted to even dream, and certainly too exhausted to wake in the night, even with the cold and the sounds of the storm. Even then, as I opened my eyes, my limbs were so heavy I could hardly make them move, and I was only vaguely interested in where I was. Cisco snored softly at my shoulder, his body heat like an electric blanket, and that was all that mattered.

Finally, I forced myself to snake one hand out of the warm cocoon of the sleeping bag and into the cold air of the tent—which was not, in fact, nearly as cold as I had expected it to be. Cisco opened his eyes and gazed at me, but did not volunteer to get up. I pressed firmly against the side of the tent, and then, sitting up, I pushed against the top, where ice crystals had formed from the condensation of our breath during the night. The canvas was as rigid as rock. Snow had buried the tent and created a virtual igloo. From the silence that surrounded us, I thought the storm was over. But we were sealed inside.

The first temptation was to stay there. The snow was insulating and we had everything we needed inside. The thought of leaving the warm sleeping bag was excruciating. But when I thought about how the others might have endured the night, particularly Paul, dread twisted like an icicle in my belly, and I knew I had to get out and survey the damage.

Cisco yawned loudly as I unzipped the sleeping bag, stretched, and shook out his coat, ready to face the day. I splashed some water into his bowl from the bottle I had kept warm in the sleeping bag, and he lapped it up happily while I pulled on my boots and gloves. I unzipped the flap of the tent and opened it on a block of solid snow.

I took my camp shovel from my backpack and started digging. The snow was soft and easy to move, and it didn't take long for Cisco to catch on and start digging too. We broke through to a pale daylight after only a few minutes. The snow was still falling in slow, fat flakes, but the wind had stopped and the sky had lost its angry look. All around was a still white landscape of blue shadowed snow, as pretty as a Christmas card — and just as featureless. No landmarks, no trail, no footprints. No tents.

Cisco bounded out and immediately foundered to his chest in the snow. The expression on his face would have been comical under other circumstances. He paddled forward a few steps, then began to dive like a porpoise through the sea of snow. I waded out up to my knees, trying to get my bearings, and I noticed Cisco was digging in the snow a few feet to the right of me. I got to him as quickly as possible, feeling my boot knock against a ground stake when I reached him. I had found Paul's tent.

I scooped away armfuls of snow and had the flap clear in a matter of moments. Apparently the meager heat of the camp stove had mitigated the accumulation of snow on his tent, which was both a good and a bad thing. I reached down to unzip the frozen zipper and had to push Cisco away in order to reach it. That was when I realized what had attracted Cisco's attention to the tent in the first place. There was a darkish stain at the bottom of the tent canvas, and when I brushed away more snow, I saw red.

"Paul?"

I unzipped the tent to let in light, and I saw the red stain was in fact a frozen puddle of blood. Paul Evans lay stiff and unmoving in the middle of it, his eyes open, a gaping black fissure splitting his skull from ear to crown. He was dead.

CHAPTER NINETEEN

etective Ritchie passed me a piece of paper. "Can you draw a map of the camp site for me, showing the location of each person's tent? Put the initials of the occupant on each tent."

I did, and returned the paper to him.

"You said the tents were only a couple of feet apart."

"That's right."

"And you were alone when you discovered the body."

"Yes."

"Where was the hatchet?"

"I don't know. I don't remember who had it last, and we never saw it again."

Agent Brown said, "So let me see if I've got the sequence of events right. You were the first one down the rope, am I right?"

"Yes."

"And Paul Evans was still alive at that point."

"Yes."

"You're sure."

"Yes."

"When you heard the dog barking, did you run to meet the others?"

"No. I couldn't see them. I took out my whistle and so did Jess. We blew our whistles to guide them." I couldn't prevent a note of pride in my voice as I added, "Cisco led them right to us."

"And you put up his tent and unpacked his pack without any assistance."

"I didn't actually unpack anything. I made sure he had food and water, and put down a ground cover and wrapped him in his sleeping bag. That's all."

"And the hatchet."

"What?"

"You took the hatchet."

"I told you. We needed it to pound down

the stakes."

"But earlier you stated you hadn't handled the hatchet."

I foundered. "I meant—what I meant was… not until later. Not until we all did, to secure the tent stakes."

"Would you say that the wound that killed Paul Evans, the one that, as you said, split open his skull, was probably made by that hatchet?"

Sonny said, "My client won't be answering that."

Mr. Willis added, "If we can't keep the questions to Miss Stockton's actual experience, I'm afraid we'll have to end this."

Agent Brown was unaffected. "You stated that when you got up the snow was pristine. No footprints, no sign the snow had been disturbed in any way?"

"No." I swallowed hard. "Whoever… whatever happened must have been fairly soon after we all went to our tents. The bloodstains were under ten or twelve inches of snow."

He nodded. "So you're saying the murder occurred shortly after you put Paul Evans in his tent and took the hatchet."

I stared at him, even as Sonny replied, "That's not what she's saying at all."

I said, "Are you implying something?"

"Your tent was here." He turned the map I had drawn around to face me and tapped the position of the little triangle marked *R.S.* "To the right of Evans's, two feet away."

"That's right."

"But you didn't hear or see anyone moving to or from his tent."

"I was asleep. There was a blizzard outside. I was inside my tent. No, I didn't see or hear anyone."

"And your dog? Wouldn't he have barked if someone came that close to your tent?"

My tone was cold. "Only if he heard them. He doesn't have supernatural powers. There was a blizzard."

Detective Ritchie said, "When you came out that morning you said all the tents were covered with snow. You couldn't see them, is that right?"

"That's right."

"Suggesting you were the first one to leave his or her tent after the blizzard struck."

I said, "Heather came out a few minutes after I did."

He made a note of that. "Would you be surprised if the blood on your jacket tested out to match that of Paul Evans?"

Sonny said impatiently, "Oh, for God's sake."

I spoke over her, sharply, "No, I wouldn't be surprised, since he bled all over me while I was helping get him down that cliff. Everyone on that mountain had blood on their clothes when we were rescued. Are you going to test them all?"

He replied matter of factly, "That's precisely what we're going to do."

Agent Brown looked up from his note-taking, his expression somber and, for the first time, mildly sympathetic. I was immediately suspicious. "Miss Stockton, I can't imagine what you went through out there. Your actions were heroic. You hadn't signed up for this, but you took upon yourself the lives of five children and three adults, one of who was severely injured and a dangerous drain on your resources. Moreover, he was all but a proven child molester and possibly a murderer, whose own wife had turned her back on him. And, let's be honest, for all your efforts to keep him alive, everyone in your party would have been better off if he had died, am I right?"

I stared at him. My voice was hoarse when I said, "What did you say?"

He replied mildly, "No one is here to judge you, Miss Stockton. Lives were depending on you. Paul Evans had virtually no chance of survival, and even if he lived, it would only be to face the justice system which, I'll be the first to admit, hasn't exactly proven itself just in the past few years."

"I risked my life to save him!"

"No one is denying that," he agreed. "But when other lives were at stake—innocent lives—what happened?"

I couldn't speak. All I could do was stare at him.

"So what happened next?" prompted Agent Brown. "Please be specific about the details."

I said abruptly, "I need to go to the ladies room."

Detective Ritchie responded immediately, as any gentlemen would to such a request, "Of course." He lifted his arm in a gesture to the mirrored panel over my shoulder and I realized for the first time that people were watching us from behind it. I should have known that, I just hadn't cared before. "I'll get a policewoman to escort you."

"I don't need an escort," I snapped back. "I've been going to the bathroom by myself since I was three years old."

Sonny pushed herself to her feet. "I'll go with you, Raine."

I could tell the two policemen didn't like it, but just like that, she had transformed an officer-of-the-court-escorting-a-suspect into two girls visiting the ladies' room on their break, and no one dared call her on it.

I did not notice the corridors, the glass-doored offices, the ringing phones, the officers moving back and forth or the voices. If I had been required to find my way back by myself, I would not have been able to do so. I walked with my head down, eyes focused on the polished industrial linoleum, my arms folded and my fingers digging into my biceps to keep the shivers from wracking my whole body. "They think I did it," I said lowly, in a tight voice. I did not look at Sonny so she wouldn't know how scared I was. "They actually think I had something to do with it."

Sonny was checking her phone messages. "No one thinks that, Raine. They're just trying to find out what happened. They're asking everyone the same questions."

"I risked my life climbing down that cliff!"

"I know that. Everyone knows that."

"They make it sound like—like some kind of Donner Party thing went on there, like people really make those kinds of decisions, like anyone would really do that!"

We had reached the door with the word "Women" stenciled on it, and Sonny stopped. She did not answer, and I looked at her. She said gently, "Raine, someone did."

I wanted to say something in reply, but I couldn't. I felt my throat start to tighten up. I pushed open the door of the ladies' room and left her behind.

Inside the stall, I dropped my head to my knees and sobbed silently until I couldn't get my breath.

~

I washed my face in cold water and finger-combed my tangled hair. There was nothing I could do about my red, swollen eyes or my cracked lips. I met Sonny in the hall, where she was just finishing a phone call. She was smiling before she looked at me. "Maude says to assure you all is well, but if you need her to drive up, she is ready and able."

But when she turned to me her expression changed, and her eyes were immediately flooded with compassion. "Raine, we can stop this. We'll come back tomorrow. You're exhausted."

I said tiredly, "You know what I was thinking the whole time? Well, a lot of the time. How easy it would have been for me to end up like one of those kids. There's no reason I didn't. No logic to it, really. The luck of the draw. It could have been me at the mercy of someone like Paul Evans."

"But it wasn't." She looked at me closely. "Is there something you want to tell me? Now would be the time."

I said softly, almost to myself, "I just can't figure it out. Why not me?" I squared my shoulders. "Make sure Cisco gets home to Maude," I said. "She's the only one who knows about his diet."

"You can take him home yourself."

"I don't want him to spend another night in a cage. You know how he hates to be crated."

"Raine, honestly…"

"Promise me." I looked at her, holding on to my composure with both hands. "Just in case."

She looked as though she wanted to argue, but then her expression softened, and she touched my arm. "Don't worry," she said. "I'll take care of it."

I relaxed marginally, and took a breath. "Okay. Let's get this done."

CHAPTER TWENTY

Heather had cleared a passage out of her tent when I pulled a blanket over Paul's face and left him, zipping his tent securely behind me. Cisco bounded over to Heather and she bent to greet him. I plowed my way over to her more slowly, and spoke briefly in a low tone.

"Paul is dead," I said.

Nothing but dismay registered in her face, and she rose slowly. "Oh, my God. Oh, no."

"Where is the hatchet?"

"What?" she looked confused. "I don't know who had it last. Why?"

"Because Paul didn't die of his injuries. Someone gashed his head open."

She looked at me for a moment without comprehension, then the color began to drain from her face. "What?"

But the snow was still falling, we were still stranded, and the shock and horror that had seized my gut when I saw Paul had turned to a knot of terror as I looked around for the other tents. "We have to check on the others," I said, stumbling back in the direction of my tent.

"I can't even see the tents!" Heather cried.

"Start with your own and work yourself around. Cisco, with me!"

I started screaming then, "Jess! Pete! Girls! Yell so I can find you! Blow your whistles!"

After a moment I heard some faint noise, and Cisco bounded toward it. I started digging and so did he, and in a moment we had cleared the snow from the entrance of Tiffanie's tent. She stumbled out into the snowy day and looked around in awe. Heather was helping Lourdes crawl out of her tent. Tiffanie said in a small voice, "Oh my God. Look at this. Just look at it. Is it an avalanche? Are we going to die?"

"We're not going to die," I said. "Grab your shovel. "Help me find the others."

With four of us plus Cisco working, it only took a few minutes to free the others. But when Heather and Jess dug the snow away from Rachel's tent, they found it empty.

I went to check for myself and found her backpack gone as well. There was no sign of the hatchet.

I crawled back out and stood up, beckoning the others to come close. They huddled around looking miserable and scared, but also a little excited, the way young people tend to do when in the midst of an adventure. They were all battered and worn, their clothing torn and stained with mud and soot and blood from yesterday's harrowing climb down into the gorge. I didn't know how to tell them what I had to tell them, but I didn't give myself much time to think about either.

I said, squinting against the snow that battered my face, "I have some bad news. Mr. Evans died during the night." I didn't think there was any reason to say more, and I met Heather's gaze in a warning. I heard some soft sounds of horror from some of the girls—I don't know which ones—and Jess swore shortly, stuffing his hands into his pockets and hunching his shoulders. Everyone looked at the zippered tent where Paul Evans' body lay, and I thought about the way they had all lined up against me yesterday when I asked them to help me. They did not look angry or defiant now. They looked stunned and lost and disbelieving. They looked like children alone and scared in the woods.

I said, because I thought they had heard

enough bad news for one day, "Mrs. Evans has gone for help." Maybe she had. But I doubted it. "In the meantime, we're on our own. We need to cut some of those evergreen boughs for a wind shelter and dig out some branches to make a fire. Who has the hatchet?"

They looked from one to the other. No one spoke up.

"Come on, guys, I'm not kidding. We've got to find it."

But we never did.

~

The snow fell for another four hours. We managed to get a small, sputtering fire going of wet sticks and brambles, just enough to melt the water that was left in our canteens. I felt guilty for thinking it, but I wished I had not wasted the fuel in my camp stove on Paul the previous night. It might well have proven the difference between life and death to us over the coming days.

I felt guilty for a lot of things. For causing the delay at the bridge. For sending the kids down the footpath into the gorge without knowing whether we would be able to get out. For putting my phone in my backpack instead of my pocket. If anyone wanted to know whose fault this was, the answer was clear: It was mine.

And I felt guilty every time I looked at Lourdes, because all I could remember was the way she had stood on the bridge with the phone in her hand and shouted, "You're going to pay!" Had she made sure of it, sometime during that night? I felt guilty when I looked at Heather because all I could see was the hatchet in her hand, when I had passed it to her last night. I felt guilty when I looked at Jess, because he had come back to help me, but the hatred in his eyes when he had looked at Paul Evans yesterday had chilled my soul. I felt guilty because before this morning I could not have imagined that a high school student could take a hatchet and split an injured man's skull while he slept. And because, when I tried to imagine what they had endured at Paul Evans's hands, I had a hard time passing judgment on any of them.

When a couple of hours had passed and Rachel still had not returned, I made a decision. I called the group together. "We're breaking camp," I told them. "We're almost out of water and we don't have enough dry wood to melt the snow it would take to make drinking water for us all. There's no way of knowing how much worse the weather is going to get. If we can get out of the gorge we can make it to the lodge in a day. But we've got to get out of the gorge."

"What about Mrs. Evans?" Angel said.

I had no ready answer for that. Part of me hoped we would find her. Another part hoped we would not, because I didn't think she could have survived the night out in that storm.

Heather volunteered, "Maybe she'll meet us at the lodge."

Pete looked around uneasily. "I don't see the path out of here, do you?"

"We'll find it," I assured him.

But I had no idea how.

~

I planted a stake wrapped in orange emergency tape to mark the site of Paul's tent, and left the body inside. I didn't know what else to do. My priority was to take care of the ones who were still alive and to try to keep them that way.

There is nothing more exhausting than wading through knee-deep snow without snowshoes and carrying the weight of a backpack, and our progress was excruciatingly slow. I strapped on Cisco's rubber booties to keep the weight of the snow between his paw pads from slowing him down, but even his customary exuberance was tempered. My heart began to pound after half an hour, and I worried about Lourdes. But no one considered leaving her behind this time. When she began to stagger, Tiffanie silently took her backpack and carried it for a while. When Tiffanie tired, she passed it to Pete, and so on throughout the day.

I had a picture in my head of where I had spotted the footpath in relationship to the bridge yesterday, and my plan was to hike until I could get a clear view of the bridge, then navigate a course toward the general direction in which I remembered the footpath lay. We had been traveling about three hours before I realized that the reason I couldn't see the bridge was because it was not there anymore.

The gorge was filled with uneven shelves and unexpected drop-offs, slow hills and steep slides. Already Pete had made a misstep and ended up in a hole with snow up to his chest. Heather had landed hard on a declination and had been limping ever since. I had noticed that the snow level had been decreasing for some time now and hoped that meant we had reached a slope that would eventually lead up and out of the gorge. But I had no way of knowing.

I stood at the top of a small incline—the reason I knew this was because the snow was only up to my ankles—and gazed at the torn and twisted support post at the top of the gorge that was now only half-visible beneath a massive fallen tree. The snow had stopped, but the day was still overcast, and doubtless I would not have noticed it at all if one of the guide wires had not suddenly flapped in a gust of wind. My heart sank.

The others drew up beside me, exhausted, breathing hard. I pointed wordlessly.

"Man," Jess said softly, and for a moment we all just stood there in a kind of numb stupefaction, marveling over what nature had wrought.

I turned in a slow circle, trying to get my bearings. Cisco, his hiking lead still attached to my waist, wandered in front of me, sniffing the snow-covered ground. And it all happened at once. The snow embankment beneath me gave way and I started to fall. Someone screamed. I saw a yellow blur of fur. I landed on my belly, frantically clawing at the snow as I continued to slide, and then my forward momentum was abruptly halted. Someone had caught my feet.

There was a lot of shouting:

"I've got her, I've got her!"

"Don't let go!'

"Hold on!"

"Oh my God, the dog!"

That was when I looked down and saw Cisco, about six feet below me, clawing at the snow for purchase, hanging by his neck from the end of the leash. I had been carrying his backpack the last half hour or so, when he had begun to stagger beneath its weight, and had automatically transferred the leash clip from his backpack harness to his buckle collar. I was hanging upside-down halfway over the drop off, but the fall had sent him tumbling down before me. The leash was still attached to me, and the more he struggled, the more precarious both our positions became.

I screamed: "*Cisco!*" And flung out my arms for him. The minute I did I began to slip further over the edge. There was more screaming from above me. I felt more hands on my legs, and someone grabbed the bottom of my coat. I heard desperate wheezing sounds coming from Cisco's throat and I saw the whites of his eyes. It was a chillingly eerie echo of the moment he had fallen over the cliff on the second day of the hike, only this time my worst nightmare was coming true. He was going to die.

I sobbed, "Cisco, here!"

He tried. He couldn't make it.

One of the boys said, "I can't get a grip! She's too far over!"

"Let me go!" I cried. "Let me go!"

Someone else said, "Cut the rope!"

"No!"

"Let him go!"

"No!"

"You're choking him, man! He's dying!"

Someone sobbed, "Cisco!"

I screamed, "Don't!"

But suddenly the tension on the leash was released and Cisco tumbled away from me, the leash that had once been attached to my waist lashing through the air after him.

I was still screaming when they pulled me over the ledge. I saw a blur of terrified faces, but immediately scrambled back to the edge, frantically searching for Cisco. I heard Lourdes cry, "There he is!" She dropped down beside me just as I saw a snowball about twelve feet below transform itself into a golden retriever who wrestled himself to his feet and shook off his coat. My heart started to beat again. "He's okay!"

The joy in her face reflected my own relief and was echoed in the sea of dirty, pinched, brave and suddenly hopeful faces that surrounded me. Jess and Pete punched each other on the arms, grinning. Angel and Tiffanie hugged each other. Heather hugged them both. "He's okay! He's okay!" And it was as though they were saying *We're okay! We're all going to be okay!*

I hugged Lourdes. "Thanks, you guys." I was trying not to cry. "Thanks. You were great."

Angel said, "How're we going to get him back up here?"

I looked down again. I couldn't tell whether what Cisco had tumbled into was a stream bed or a natural depression in the gorge, but its walls were sheer and rocky, with no natural access. Cisco was sniffing the snow-covered ground, and I noticed that the snow at the bottom was barely over his paws, which was a good sign. The drift that had fooled us into thinking it was solid had apparently consisted of all the blown snow from the night before.

I said, "Ropes. I'll go over and—"

Before I finished speaking I saw Jess's face fall.

We had used all our ropes on the descent into the gorge, and they were still tied to a tree on the upper rim. I said quickly, "It's okay. We'll figure something out. Let me think."

I turned back to Cisco and called him. He was circling the ground with his nose to the snow, dragging his leash, and when he heard my voice he looked up, but immediately returned his attention to the snow, pawing at the ground.

"What's he doing?" Lourdes said.

"He's found something." Tiffanie peered over my shoulder.

Heather said, "What—?" And then she stopped, her eyes filled with reluctant horror as they met mine. "You don't suppose... could it be Mrs. Evans?"

Everyone crowded close to the ledge then, watching Cisco paw the ground the way people watch the Jaws of Life cut open a crushed automobile on the highway. Angel and Tiffanie clutched each other's hands. No one spoke. I didn't want to speak, but I had to. It was my job... and Cisco's.

"Cisco," I said, "Find."

He began to dig with both paws. Snow flew. He thrust his nose into the snow, sneezed and shook his head, and dug some more. The next time he pushed his muzzle into the snow, he came up with something in his mouth. I held my breath until I saw what it was.

It was a phone. My phone.

"Oh my God," breathed Heather. "Do you think it still works? Could it possibly still work?"

I called, "Cisco, good boy, good find! Cisco, here!"

Swishing his tail proudly, Cisco marched to the bottom of the embankment and leapt up a few feet, then skidded back down. The phone was still in his mouth. He tried again. This time he made it a little higher, but slid down before he could gain purchase.

I shrugged out of my backpack. "Okay, you're going to have to lower me over the edge. Somebody find me a long branch or stick—five or six feet. Hurry!" and then, "Cisco, wait!"

Cisco stopped flinging himself at the bank and backed off, swinging his tail uncertainly, still holding onto the phone. The kids scrambled to find a broken branch, all the while demanding, "What are you going to do? How can you pull him up with this?"

"Hold onto my legs," I said, and, grabbing the

long, crooked stick, I slithered carefully over the edge.

"Cisco," I called down to him, "Here!"

He lunged at the bank again, and this time I swung the stick downward to catch the end of his leash. I twisted the stick around until the fabric of the leash caught, ever so precariously, in the fork of the stick. Working quickly and carefully, I pulled the stick back toward me, and when Cisco started to slide down again I jerked the stick upward until I could grab the end of the leash. "Good boy!" I called to Cisco. I was gasping with exertion and my arms were trembling, but I held on fast. "Pull me back!" I called over my shoulder and to Cisco, "Cisco, scramble! Good dog! Scramble!"

Inch by excruciating inch, I guided Cisco up the bank while my teammates held on to my coat, my boots and my belt to keep me from tumbling over. My shoulders were screaming with pain, my kneecaps had gone numb, and the leash was wound so tightly around my hand that I couldn't feel my fingers anymore. But when Cisco's face was within inches of mine, when he was close enough for me to grab his collar and haul him over the edge I collapsed backwards, shaking and gasping for breath. The kids cheered and descended on Cisco, hugging him and rubbing his fur and slapping his shoulders. I pried the phone from Cisco's mouth before throwing my own arm around his neck, rubbing my forehead against his. "Good dog," I kept saying, over and over again. "Good, good dog."

When the phone began to vibrate in my hand at first I didn't feel it, or understand what it meant. Then I opened my palm and stared at the flashing blue screen in disbelief. Lourdes must have turned it on when she was brandishing it in front of Paul on the bridge. It might even have been the sound of the vibration that had attracted Cisco to dig for it, or it might have been the memory of the peanut butter that had been smeared on the last phone he found.

Everyone went silent, staring, with me, at the miracle of technology that buzzed in my hand. Then someone cried, "Answer it!"

Convulsively, I pushed the "Speak" button.

"Raine, for God's sake," Miles said shortly, "I know you're angry with me but you're acting like a child." His voice was broken with static and fading fast. "I've—been—two days. You—"

"Miles," I gasped hoarsely. I wanted to weep with relief for the sound of his voice, and maybe I did. "Miles we need help—"

"What? I can't hear—"

"We're in trouble!" I cried. "We're trapped, and Paul is dead—"

"Raine—fading…. Where…"

The screen went black, and there was nothing but dead air.

CHAPTER TWENTY-ONE

For a moment there was silence in the room. Everyone looked at me, waiting for me to finish. But they knew how it ended. "We were too exhausted to go any farther," I said. "And too defeated. When the phone died, it was like everyone just gave up. We found a place to make camp a few hundred feet away. The next morning we heard the rescue helicopters. I guess the phone still had enough juice to transmit the GPS coordinates to Miles when he called."

Ritchie nodded. "It did. Mr. Young did everything but call out the National Guard, and I'm not too sure he wouldn't have managed that too if you hadn't been found when you were. Quite an adventure you had there, Miss Stockton. One question."

But he turned suddenly at the sound of the opening door. My own ears heard nothing but panting breath and scrambling claws, and I gave a cry of joy as I jumped up from the table and ran to embrace my dog. "Cisco!"

Buck let the leash drop and Cisco ran to me. I almost overturned my chair in my hurry to get to him, dropping to the floor and flinging my arms around his neck. He smelled of antiseptic and warm fur and simple, unadulterated love. He tried to climb into my lap, he was so happy to see me, and I just sat there on the floor, hugging him, for the longest time.

I heard Ritchie say, "Sheriff, I thought we agreed you were to watch from the observation room."

And then I heard another familiar voice: "We got bored. How the hell are you, Ritch?"

"Uncle Roe!" I jumped to my feet and flung myself on my uncle, burying my face in his wool sweater while he patted my back soothingly, just like he used to do when I was a child.

I stepped away from him, searching his face in astonishment and delight. "What are you doing here? How did you—?"

"Don't be silly, Rainbow, did you think I'd leave you by yourself up here? Your aunt would have my hide."

I turned to Buck. "I thought you were in Florida."

He shrugged and gave a faint smile. He looked

weary and strained, his strong good looks fading against the stress of the past days. "This is my case, you know. The whole thing started in my county."

I wanted to hug him, to touch him. He had been my husband for so long, and he was here now, when I needed him most. But he belonged to someone else now. The moment was awkward and aching.

Cisco had made his waggy-tailed round of the table and now pressed his shoulder against my knee. I said softly to Buck, "I'm so sorry about your mother."

He nodded and touched my arm. "I know."

Then he turned to Detective Ritchie. "We just got word that the search team found a body that they believe to be Rachel Evans. The apparent cause of death was exposure. Her coat was covered with blood, which I suspect you'll find matches that of the murder victim."

Uncle Roe added, "They also bagged as evidence a hatchet that she had in her backpack. I believe the men on the scene said there were stains on the blade that looked suspicious."

Another man came in behind my uncle and handed detective Ritchie a stack of folders. He spoke lowly but I heard him say, "So far the statements are consistent. Here's the coroner's prelim. Looks like the hatchet is the murder weapon."

I felt a little woozy. I sank to the floor again, burying my face in Cisco's coat, because I wasn't entirely certain how much longer my knees would support me.

The two investigators shuffled the file folders between them for what seemed like endless moments, opening them, reading the contents, conferring in mutters over a page or two. Then Agent Brown glanced at Detective Ritchie. "Well, then. That's that." He closed his notebook. "I'll hang around until we get the rest of the statements, but I think I've got all I need here."

Sonny stood up and extended her hand to him. "Nice to meet you, Special Agent Brown." She offered her hand to Detective Ritchie. "Detective." She turned to Mr. Willis. "Is there any place open for lunch, do you think?"

I lifted my head as the two attorneys began to pack their briefcases. Just like that, it was all over and everyone was friends. I stood slowly, winding Cisco's leash around my hand.

Detective Ritchie said to me pleasantly, "We'll let you know if we need anything more, Miss

Stockton. Meantime, why don't you go on home and get some rest? Roe, Buck, let's get a cup of coffee and see where we stand on this thing."

Buck said, "In a minute."

Agent Brown and Detective Ritchie left the room with my uncle, and I turned in bewilderment to Sonny. "That's it?"

She smiled. "That's it. If anything else comes up they will let Bryson or me know. Meanwhile, don't talk to the press—and believe me, this will be a story. It may take a few months before all the details are ironed out, but since the prime suspect in both the Maddox incident and in the death of Paul Evans is dead herself, I really don't see how much further this can go." She glanced at Mr. Willis. "Do you?"

He said, "I believe our job here is done." He smiled and extended his hand to me. "It's been a pleasure, Miss Stockton. And Cisco." He looked down at Cisco, and Cisco, hearing his name, grinned back up at him. "It's not often I get a chance to meet a real hero."

I shook his hand, still feeling a little stunned. "Thank you. Thank you for everything."

He replied, "I'm not the one you should thank."

I knew he was right.

Sonny said, "Come have lunch with us, Raine. Do you need a ride home?"

Buck glanced at her. "I think we've got that covered."

I said to Sonny, "I figured it out."

She looked puzzled.

"Before... when I said I couldn't understand why I hadn't turned out like those kids. I figured it out." I smiled, though it was an effort. "This is why. You, flying in from the coast in a storm. And Buck coming back from Florida on a moment's notice. And Uncle Roe, and even Maude, ready to drive through a blizzard because I was in trouble. My folks may be gone but I've still got family. That's the difference."

Sonny's expression softened and she stepped forward, embracing me. My lashes were wet when we parted. She said, smiling, "See you at home."

When they were gone I was left alone with Buck. I opened my mouth to say something, I don't know what, but he touched my arm and gestured toward the door. "I'll walk you out," he said.

Cisco trotted happily between us as we moved into the corridor, unconcerned with the strange noises and smells as long as his two favorite people were with him. That's the great thing about dogs;

their needs are simple and their memories short. Cisco was going home, and as long as he got to sleep by my side at night, I doubted very much whether he would have nightmares about what had happened on the mountain.

But I would never forget it.

I said quietly to Buck, "Thanks for getting Cisco. I was so worried."

"Hey, it's the least I could do for my best bud, right, Cisco?"

Cisco trotted a little lighter and swished his tail.

"I can't believe you came all the way up here in the snow."

He answered, more solemnly, "It was the least I could do."

He touched my arm and turned me toward a corridor I didn't recognize. "There are some folks I thought you'd like to say good-bye to," he said.

A group of people was standing around a set of vending machines. Intermixed among the adults I didn't recognize were some very familiar faces. I dropped Cisco's leash and he rushed forward. So did I.

We didn't say anything. We just hugged. Lourdes. Tiffanie. Angel. Pete. Jess. Even Heather. Our embraces were hard and fierce and born of the things we had endured that no one else would ever share. They each were different people now than they had been five days ago. So was I.

It was only when it came time to say good-bye to Cisco that the party became exuberant. They rubbed his fur and patted his sides and hugged his neck and called him "little dude" and "golden baby" and "the best dog ever," and they clung to him so long that I felt bad when at last I took his leash to go. Some of the parents wanted to thank me, and others just wanted to touch me, too emotional to speak. I didn't know what to say to them. I was a little emotional too.

It wasn't until we were walking back toward the lobby area that Buck said, "That's Cisco's hiking leash, isn't it? Is that the same one he was wearing when you fell?"

I nodded. "I only have one."

"Because I couldn't help noticing it has been cut."

I said nothing, and I didn't look at him.

"A normal person, listening to your statement, would assume that someone unfastened the leash from your waist. But when the kids were yelling, 'cut the rope' they knew they could, didn't they? What do you suppose they used?"

I looked straight ahead. "I couldn't see."

"I guess they could have gotten your knife."

"I guess."

"But it would have taken a long time to saw through the leash."

I did not reply.

"There was more than one hatchet on that expedition, wasn't there, Raine? I'm guessing both of the hike leaders would have had one. Or maybe Heather." He glanced at me briefly. "It only makes sense. The one that was found with Rachel was probably the murder weapon. But the other one, Paul's hatchet... I wouldn't be surprised if some camper found it someday, not far from where you guys were picked up."

I said stiffly, "I told you, I didn't see anything."

"Sure. You couldn't have, from your position. And none of the statements mention a second hatchet." He slid another glance at me. "Guess those kids learned the meaning of team work after all."

I determinedly remained silent.

He shrugged. "It's probably just as well. The existence of two hatchets would only cloud the investigation, cast suspicion on innocent people, maybe even call for a murder trial. And we have the murderer." He paused a beat. "Don't we?"

I said softly, "Those kids have been through enough."

He stopped, and this time I met his gaze. I did so without shame or regret, and we looked at each other for a long time. Then he said, "I guess you all have."

He lifted a hand as though to stroke my hair, or perhaps even draw me into an embrace. My breath stopped, just for a moment, as I looked at him, and waited. And then his gaze noticed something behind me, and his hand fell innocently to my shoulder. He nodded toward the glass door that led to the lobby. "Someone is waiting for you. I'll see you later."

He turned and went back down the hall, and I pushed through the lobby door.

I thought my chest would explode with joy when Melanie sprang from one of the chairs by the window and flung herself upon me. Cisco barked with delight. I laughed out loud. Melanie said, "I'm sorry I was a brat on the telephone. I'm glad you're okay. We got to ride in a helicopter to get here! Pepper couldn't come, though. Dad said she would throw up."

I smiled over her shoulder at her father, who

stood waiting patiently, and who made my heart soar for an entirely different reason. I gave Melanie a hard hug and then took her face between my hands. "Do you know how much your daddy loves you?" I demanded.

She was sanguine. "Sure."

"And if you ever want to talk about things—you know, girl stuff—you can come to me, right?"

She looked puzzled. "Yeah, okay."

I hugged her again and told her, "You were a brat. But I forgive you."

Melanie turned to Cisco, who was nudging her insistently for attention. "Hey, Cisco! I brought you some dog biscuits."

I laughed as I stood, leaving Cisco in Melanie's capable hands. "Music to his ears," I said.

I walked into the arms of her father and lay my head on his shoulder. "Thank you," I said, trying not to choke up.

"You're welcome." I felt the touch of his lips on my tangled hair, his hands strong on my back, gently cupping my neck. I wanted to stay like that forever, safe in his embrace.

"Are you ready to go home?" he asked.

I murmured, "I'd rather go to St. Bart's."

He stepped back and touched my chin with his

fingers, tilting my head upward so that I could look into his smiling eyes. "That," he assured me, "can be arranged."

"Say, Dad," Melanie said, bringing Cisco over to us, "aren't you afraid Cisco will throw up on the helicopter?"

I laughed, and Miles said, "Cisco is a hero. He's allowed."

I took Cisco's leash in one hand, and Melanie's hand in the other. "Come on," I said. "Let's go home."

And home, when I finally got there, had never looked so good.

Donna Ball

Also in The Raine Stockton Dog Mystery Series

SMOKY MOUNTAIN TRACKS

A child has been kidnapped and abandoned in the mountain wilderness. Her only hope is Raine Stockton and her young, untried tracking dog Cisco...

RAPID FIRE

Raine and Cisco are brought in by the FBI to track a terrorist ...a terrorist who just happens to be Raine's old boyfriend.

GUN SHY

Raine rescues a traumatized service dog, and soon begins to suspect he is the only witness to a murder.

BONE YARD:a novella

Cisco digs up human remains in Raine's back yard, and mayhem ensues. Could this be evidence of a serial killer, a long-unsolved mass murder, or something even more sinister... and closer to home?

SILENT NIGHT

It's Christmastime in Hansonville, N.C., and Raine and Cisco are on the trail of a missing teenager. But when a newborn is abandoned in the manger of the town's living nativity and Raine walks in on what appears to be the scene of a murder, the holidays take a very dark turn for everyone concerned.

Spine-chilling suspense by Donna Ball

SHATTERED

A missing child, a desperate call for help in the middle of the night... is this a cruel hoax, or the work of a maniacal serial killer who is poised to strike again?

NIGHT FLIGHT

She's an innocent woman who knows too much. Now she's fleeing through the night without a weapon and without a phone, and her only hope for survival is a cop who's willing to risk his badge—and his life—to save her.

SANCTUARY

They came to the peaceful, untouched mountain wilderness of Eastern Tennessee seeking an escape from the madness of modern life. But when they built their luxury homes in the heart of virgin forest they did not realize that something was there before them... something ancient and horrible; something that will make them believe that monsters are real.

The Dead Season

~

ABOUT THE AUTHOR....

Donna Ball is the author of over a hundred novels under several different pseudonyms in a variety of genres that include romance, mystery, suspense, paranormal, western adventure, historical and women's fiction. Recent popular series include the Ladybug Farm series by Berkley Books and the Raine Stockton Dog Mystery series. Donna is an avid dog lover and her dogs have won numerous titles for agility, obedience and canine musical freestyle. She lives in a restored Victorian Barn in the heart of the Blue Ridge mountains with a variety of four-footed companions. You can contact her at http://www.donnaball.net.

CPSIA information can be obtained
at www.ICGtesting.com
Printed in the USA
LVOW08s1427240117
522002LV00001B/41/P